PRAISE F

"If you've never read a Vivian Arend book you are missing out on one of the best contemporary authors writing today."
~ *Book Reading Gals*

"LET IT RIDE is a charming, sexy and poignant story and I loved it.
~ *Dear Author*

"Brilliant, raw, imaginative, irresistible!!"
~ *Avon Romance*

"This story will keep you reading from the first page to the last one. There is never a dull moment..."
~ *Landy Jimenez*

"HOLY FREAKIN' HELL IS THIS HOT!!!"
~ *Red Hot Plus Blue Reads*

"This was my first Vivian Arend story, and I know I want more! "
~ *Red Hot Plus Blue Reads*

"Vivian Arend takes us on a sensual ride as Mitch and Anna explore her sexuality... From beginning to end this story is very hot and highly entertaining."
~ *Where the Night Kind Roam*

RIDE BABY RIDE

THOMPSON & SONS: BOOK 1

VIVIAN AREND

ALSO BY VIVIAN AREND

Six Pack Ranch
Rocky Mountain Heat
Rocky Mountain Haven
Rocky Mountain Desire
Rocky Mountain Rebel
Rocky Mountain Freedom
Rocky Mountain Romance
Rocky Mountain Retreat
Rocky Mountain Shelter
Rocky Mountain Devil
Rocky Mountain Home

Thompson & Sons
Ride Baby Ride
Rocky Ride
One Sexy Ride
Let It Ride
A Wild Ride

A full list of Vivian's print titles is available on her website

www.vivianarend.com

Original Title: Baby, Be Mine
Retitled: Ride Baby Ride
Copyright © 2014 by Arend Publishing Inc.
ISBN: 9781989507018
Edited by Anne Scott
Cover Design © Damonza
Proofed by Sharon Muha

CHAPTER 1

September, Rocky Mountain House

If any place was the epitome of a laid-back, good ol' boys, redneck tavern, Traders Pub fit the bill. Country music blared over the speakers encouraging those out for the start of the weekend to kick up their heels and let loose.

Familiar sights, all too familiar sounds.

Even more familiar was the ache in Gage Jenick's gut as Katy Thompson shimmied past, her trim body clad in nothing fancier than a pair of jeans and a western shirt, but he was still damn near drooling.

He deliberately turned his chair away and picked up his beer, the Alberta equivalent of an ostrich burying its head in the sand.

If he didn't look, she wasn't really there.

Wasn't really there, in spite of the sweet apple-blossom scent clinging to her skin that wafted over, like it did during the day while they worked together at her family's garage. How many times in the past six months had he been in the

1

middle of welding repairs or lugging tires from one rack to another, and found his mouth watering? His head turning involuntarily as she sashayed across the wide concrete space with a question regarding billing or a parts order for one of her brothers working the floor.

He hadn't always had a hard-on for his best friend's little sis. For years she'd been Katybug—the tagalong annoyance he'd tolerated for Clay's sake, and later for the sake of the baking they'd snitch from the kitchen she'd taken possession of when her mom had passed away.

It was like a switch flipped. One day she was this invisible creature, and the next?

He could still vividly picture it—months earlier when he'd stopped work for the day. He'd rounded a corner at the garage in time to see a hose burst on her.

Water sprayed everywhere as she'd struggled to catch the flailing end.

"What the hell?" Gage rushed toward Katy who stood laughing, the broken hose writhing as if it were alive. It only took a minute for him to shut off the water at the source, but that was long enough to end with them both drenched to the skin.

"Sorry, Gage." Katy hiccupped, she was laughing so hard. "Oh, Lord that was fun. Good thing it's a warm day, right?"

He turned to deliver some timely big-brother-like, smart-ass comment, and got slammed with an eye-opening lightning bolt.

Her shirt was plastered to her, revealing more than any trip to the lake or swimming hole ever had, and to his utter shock, Katybug had hips and breasts.

And nipples.

Nipples he could clearly see pressed to the front of her

soaking wet T-shirt because she didn't appear to be wearing a bra.

"I told Clay that hose needed replacing," she complained. "But, no. He insisted it could last one more summer. *Ha*."

She leaned over and dragged her hair into a bunch, squeezing out the extra moisture. God help him. His gaze dropped to her ass, the rounded curves beckoning him forward to grab hold and take a long, thorough, exploratory detour over this brand-new Katy.

His wet clothes weren't cold enough to deter his dick from waking up. And the rest of him as well.

He hadn't been looking for romance—he'd long ago sworn off connecting with anyone full-time in a forever kind of way. The last thing he needed was someone like Katy in his life.

He had to stay in control. Had promised himself to never hold too tight to anything, or anyone. Yet in that moment he wanted little Katy Thompson with something near to obsession, and that truth rocked him to his core.

She finally clued in that he hadn't said a word. She straightened, and, oh my *God*, those *breasts*— "You okay, Gage?"

No, but that wasn't an acceptable answer. He dragged his gaze from her off-limits body and mumbled something.

His brain had been mumbling ever since.

Somehow he'd kept his growing hunger hidden from her, and her brothers, which was a miracle. And his best friend?

Gage glanced across the table at Clay Thompson. At his best friend's hands that would curl into fists the size of hams at the thought of anyone hurting his baby sister. They might go back a long way, but Gage knew the truth.

3

When it came to Katy, none of the Thompson boys would hesitate for a second to knock the head off anyone who so much as breathed wrong in her direction. Then they would calmly bury the remains in their backyard. Not even he would get a reprieve.

Good thing he planned on never hurting her.

Enough time had passed that he'd come to admit he'd like to get involved with Katy. The idea still scared him to death, but maybe with the constant threat of Clay and the rest of the hulking crew keeping him in check, he could avoid becoming what he feared. If the opportunity presented itself.

You're not your past...

Laughter from the dance floor roused him, and he blinked in surprise. In spite of his good intentions, he was staring at her, soaking in every second he could of her spark of sweet, dark happiness. She was dancing with a group of her girlfriends, the four of them ignoring the guys hovering nearby in the hopes of a dance, or a grope, or maybe something more.

At least she wasn't with *him*. The shithead boyfriend, Simon.

A hard nudge into his shoulder made his entire body shake, and he braced his beer to keep it from spilling.

Clay grinned. "You're daydreaming. So eager to get out of town you can't stay awake at your own going-away party?"

Gage laughed. "Is that what this is? I thought this was a typical Friday night at Traders."

"Didn't you get the announcement?" Clay lifted the pitcher of beer in the air and offered to refill Gage's mug. "I'd get you drunk, but you probably wouldn't appreciate the long drive ahead of you with a hangover."

They fell back into a comfortable silence for a couple minutes. Clay passed the pitcher to the other Thompson boys and their friends who'd joined them.

Gage took the opportunity to examine the room. So many people he'd spent time with over the past years. He was going to miss them while he did his stint in the north working in the oilfields, but the money was too good to turn down.

And the chance to be away from temptation. Because, damn if he hadn't automatically searched her out yet again.

Clay spoke, dragging Gage's attention off the dance floor and back to safer topics. "What time are you leaving tomorrow?" he asked.

"Around ten. I don't start until Monday, so I figured I'll drive Saturday and get set up Sunday." Gage chuckled at the expression on his friend's face. "Stop looking as if I'm running away to join the circus. I'll be back in six months."

His friend grumbled. "I know, but we'll miss you around the garage. Good cheap labour is hard to find. Heck, I'd even hired someone to replace you, and not even a month later Cassidy's gone and quit. I hate working harder."

"Can't blame the man. He's got a sweet deal with his new family." Gage took in the Coleman family gathered in another corner of the pub, some of the members partnered up, some not. The man in question, Cassidy, was slow dancing with Ashley, one of his lovers. Cassidy's other partner, Travis, looked on from the side as he chatted with his brothers.

The trio's relationship wasn't typical, but it had happened, and in a way, Gage was a little jealous. Cassidy had gotten what he'd wanted and then some. In the meantime, Gage wasn't willing to rock the boat to grasp the one woman he'd been lusting after.

Running away to the north was safer for so many reasons.

Katy lifted her hands in the air, swaying from side to side to the slow music. Her best friend Janey spun her, and wholesome, happy laughter rang, something Gage loved to hear.

Although he wished he'd been the one putting that kind of smile on her face. Bringing that shine to her dark brown eyes.

One thing was missing...one good subtraction to the evening. "Where's Simon?"

An enormous grin twisted Clay's lips. "Katy dumped him."

Gage's jaw hit the table.

"I know, I'm so fucking glad." Clay spoke as softly as he could and still be heard over the loud dance music. "You have no idea how hard it was not to tell him to get the hell away from her, but she gave me such grief the last time I scared off a boyfriend..."

Gage nodded. "I remember. It wasn't pretty. In fact," he taunted, "you were damn scared, for someone who outweighs her by a good hundred pounds. I thought she was going to kick your ass into the next county."

"It's not the size of the package, it's the pressure. She might be a tiny thing, and she's so quiet most of the time, but when that girl loses it? Me and the boys wear a cup when she's pissed."

"So...you mentioned Simon," Gage prompted. Because that was the most important bit of information here. When he'd finally woken up and figured out Katy was far more than a little-sister figure, she'd already been seeing that dickwad Simon, and if the woman had been pissed about her brothers micromanaging her life, she certainly wasn't going to be any happier to have a friend of the family butting in. "They've been an item for the past six months."

"She broke up with him last Saturday after the community picnic." Clay gave him a look. "You know, the day you punched in his face?"

Gage shoved down his rising excitement at the fact Katy was once again a free agent. Instead he focused on the joys of small-town living, where everyone knew everything about everyone, which in this case explained a lot, including covering his tracks.

He'd had a good reason to punch Simon, but he'd also enjoyed the hell out of it for his own personal reasons, i.e., the ass was getting to fool around with *his* Katy. "The jerk was being a homophobic asshole."

Clay shrugged. "I'm not saying you were wrong. Katy saw the light that day as well and told him to—in her own words—crawl into a hole and rot." Clay nodded in obvious agreement with the sentiment. "I'm glad she came to her senses."

Gage's excitement shot sky-high. This was his chance. Katy was free? Other than the bad news of him leaving the next damn day... "Clay, I've been meaning to ask you something."

His friend pulled out his phone and stared at the message on the screen. "That's your 'I need a favour' voice."

Busted. "Not so much a favour as...well, I was wondering about Katy, and—"

"Damn," Clay cut in. "Yeah, can you take care of her?"

Gage jolted back. "What?"

"I just got a call for the tow truck, and I've got to take it." Clay rose to his feet then leaned over to make sure no one overheard. "Look, Katy put her car in the garage for me to do a service checkup. I didn't get a chance to look at it yet so

I offered to drive tonight and be her DD. Now I have to bail, so could you give her a ride home?"

It was like being handed the keys to paradise and told not to unlock the gate. Gage nodded. "I'll get her home safe."

He might go to hell along the way, but it would be worth it.

Gage was watching her.

Katy allowed the hope inside to rise. Every time she'd checked, his gaze had been pinned on her body. Her hips, her chest—and it wasn't creepy as if he were some kind of stalker. And it wasn't whacko or possessive like her now-ex-boyfriend Simon had been for the last month or so.

Nope, what she saw was all-out admiration, especially since she was watching his reflection in the mirror, and he had no idea she knew what he was doing.

Her best friend caught her hand and tugged her closer. "You want a drink?" Janey asked.

"Sure." Katy took one final peek to reassure herself even as she tried to figure out the best way to make a move.

Because the crush she'd had on the man had been going on far, far too long. Since she'd been in her teens. Clay had dragged the new kid home after school years earlier, so when her hormones had woken up, he'd already been firmly underfoot. Gage was one of the never-ending kids fostered by the friendly couple down the block, but he'd been the only one to walk through the Thompson doors and never really leave.

Janey headed straight for the Thompson table—which Katy should have expected. "Hi, Len."

Katy's third oldest brother blinked in surprise as Janey interrupted his conversation. Not only that, she grabbed a chair and basically shoved her way between the guys, settling in like she belonged.

Katy twisted away to hide her smile. *Janey* wasn't afraid of going after what she wanted, which in this case was Len.

A strong hand caught her arm and tugged her out of the path of a waitress carrying a loaded tray through the bar. "Sit down, Katy," Gage ordered, adjusting the chair next to him. The one Clay had been occupying.

She frowned, but obeyed. "Where's Clay?"

"Tow-truck callout."

"Great. How am I supposed to get home?"

Gage shifted in his chair. "I'll take you."

Her heart skipped a beat then rolled across the floor. He sounded more pissed than thrilled at that option. "It's okay, I'm pretty sure I can find someone else to—"

"No," Gage snapped, his dark eyes meeting hers. The square cut of his jawline held tight. He touched her again, his fingers slowly skimming down her arm. A deliberate caress that made goose bumps rise, especially as this time his voice softened to stroke her as well. "I have no problem taking you home."

Katy swallowed hard. Not only his fingers but his words slipped over her like an erotic touch. He wasn't hiding his admiration anymore—what she'd seen in the mirror was right out in the open, and *sweet mercy*...

His lips twisted into a smile. "I hear you and Simon called it quits."

"He's a pig." She spoke without thinking, but all Gage did in response was grin harder. Her mouth was dry. "I need a drink."

They reached for the same glass, and their fingers

bumped, his big hand nearly eclipsing hers as he closed his grip and teasingly helped lower the glass to the table in front of her.

"Beer? Or something else?" he asked.

"Coke."

Katy waited until he released her, but his touch had already started an electric tingle that raced from her fingertips all the way up her arm and a whole lot farther. It affected her breathing, that was for sure, and she couldn't seem to take anything more than shallow gasps.

He filled her glass from a pitcher.

"Thanks."

"No problem."

She lifted her glass in the hopes it would cool the heat that had enveloped her, but suddenly she wasn't sure she could swallow. His gaze was pinned to her lips. He'd leaned in, one hand casually resting on the back of her chair as if she were in his embrace. Around them the music continued to blast, voices rose and fell. Laughter and shouting.

The room could have been empty.

The sweet liquid stole down her throat, ice cubes bumping her lips as she stared over the rim of the glass. He adjusted position and their thighs touched. She jerked the glass back to vertical before she dropped it altogether.

Heat from his leg wrapped over hers. It took everything in her to stop from squirming in her chair to ease the pressure building inside as Gage continued to look her over as if she were the feature steak on the barbeque menu.

"I'm not drunk," she whispered.

He shifted, his leg rubbing hers, and her breath caught in her throat. "Never said you were."

"I *should* be drunk," she clarified. "Because that would explain why you're looking at me like that."

Gage eased off, glancing around the room. "How am I looking at you?"

"Like you want..." She picked up her glass and sniffed it to see if she'd accidentally gotten a double shot of rum in her coke. Anything that would explain what was going on. That would explain how this thing she'd dreamed about was really happening.

A hand settled on her thigh under the table, and she snapped to attention. Gage leaned in, turning his head at the last moment so his lips were directly next to her ear. "You're not drunk. Neither am I."

Oh, sweet Lord. She ignored him. Ignored the large palm that covered her thigh. Ignored the lust racing through her veins, and all the happy hormones that were waving pom-poms. She took another sip of her drink while he settled back in his chair, opening some distance between them.

"Katy, let's dance." Janey had her by the hand and pulled her to her feet, headed back to the floor before Katy could protest that she'd been having a lovely hallucination and she'd take a rain check on the dancing.

Only Gage didn't stop watching her. Didn't take his gaze off her, and now Katy wasn't getting sweaty on the dance floor because she was shaking her bootie hard.

It was all about Gage Jenick and his hungry eyes.

She glanced at her watch and wondered how early she could call it a night because she could hardly wait for him to take her home.

CHAPTER 2

K aty danced. Gage debated.

He was leaving within the next twelve hours. Did he really have a right to say something to her now?

On the other hand, did he want to take a chance of not saying anything only to return home and discover she'd hooked up with some other guy, and he'd be once again left bouncing his fist in frustration? Because there had been a whole lot of that going on for the past few months.

It wasn't just sexual attraction, though. If it were, he'd have somehow reined in his raging libido and not hinted that he planned to jump her bones.

Nope. He wanted more than sex. Maybe it was stupid to be thinking long-term not even thirty minutes after hearing she was available, but everything about the woman fit him so well. She was smart and entertaining, pushy enough to deal with her four brothers and yet she did so in her own soft-spoken way.

She was a hell of a package, and he wanted nothing more than to unwrap her one layer at a time and thoroughly mesh their lives together. Starting tonight. Maybe it was bad timing, but if he didn't say something he'd spend the next six months regretting it.

Also, not that he was a chicken or anything, but the time lag, *if* Katy agreed they'd be together, would give Clay time to get over any violent urges that might arise.

Would give Gage time to make sure this was going to work—that he could handle the new situation as well as he hoped. That he wasn't going to revert to...

Not going there.

Katy tumbled off the dance floor with Janey, the two of them red-cheeked and bright-eyed. They whirled to a stop, Katy only inches away from his knees as she rocked back to vertical and smiled shyly.

"You okay heading out now?" Katy asked. The slightly out-of-breath quality of her question could be excused by her recent fling around the dance floor.

He hoped it was for other reasons. "Grab your coat."

"I'm staying for *loooonger,*" Janey teased. "Because I don't have a cuuuurfew, not like some people."

"Shut up, Janey," Katy poked back. "You should go home now before your carriage turns into a pumpkin."

Janey stuck out her tongue. "I'm not driving, so there."

Gage rose to his feet to troubleshoot best he could, even distracted by his plans for the rest of the evening. "Katy, you want us to give Janey a ride home first?"

Janey pulled back with a pout, accidentally bumping Len in the process. He caught her as she swayed, arms rising in the air momentarily. "*Whooooaa.* But I'm not ready to leave," she protested.

Len and Gage exchanged glances. Len rolled his eyes, settling Janey back on her feet. "I'll make sure she gets home when she's had enough."

"Going to shut the place down," Janey warned.

Gage double-checked Katy's expression, but there was no concern there, only a bit of a smirk. He grabbed the bull by the horns and Katy by the hand, linking their fingers together. "Come on, let's go."

It took a couple minutes of dodging through the close crowd, her hand tight in his, before they were outside. Voices and music faded to a faint buzz. Distant car traffic mixed in, but there was pretty much nothing but the fresh September air and the warmth of her body as he stepped next to her and slipped an arm around her waist.

"Gage?"

He squeezed lightly. "What's up, Katybug?"

She didn't answer until they'd reached his truck, then she faced him, her head tilted to the side in this adorable manner. "I'm not sure what's going on."

Gage leaned in, one hand planted against the truck door beside her head, the other still resting on her hip. "I'm taking you home."

Her tongue snuck out, leaving her lips shining in the pale parking lights. "You look like you got more on your mind than that."

He lowered his voice. "Would you be okay with it if I did?"

Her eyes widened slightly, but she nodded.

Hallelujah. Gage closed the distance between them and touched their lips together. Soft. Sweet. More intense than any kiss he'd ever given her before—those innocent busses on the cheek during family holiday gatherings. Her breath escaped in a puff as he pulled back, warming his skin. "Oh. That was nice."

"Hmm, you ready for better than nice?"

She opened her mouth to answer, and he caught her

with her lips separated. His tongue eased into her mouth, and he tasted her like he'd longed to for months. Sweetness, a touch of cinnamon, but mostly *her*. This was far better than *nice*. He dug his fingers into the fabric at her hip to stop from exploring anywhere else. His other hand locked on the truck frame to make sure the only thing he used on her was his mouth.

He wanted to consume her. Kissing was only the beginning because, oh hell, every nerve in his body had gone on high alert. Especially when she curled her hands around his back and stepped against him. One leg on either side of his thigh. Bodies tight together, her warmth enveloping him along with the scent of her perfume. His head spun from even this much contact, his erect cock pressed to one side of her soft belly.

Stay in control.

Somehow he retreated, this time to stare into a face that held the hugest eyes—wide pupils and wet swollen lips open in an O as she gasped for air.

He didn't say another word until they were in the truck. Gage caught her by the hip and dragged her across the bench seat to his side. "Buckle up."

The question was there in her eyes, but the words never came, and he wasn't ready for them, either.

He drove with one hand, his right arm draped around her shoulders so he could snuggle her tight. Every time they stopped for a set of lights, he couldn't resist leaning over and kissing her. Each stop grew a little more intense, slowly building the need inside him. Each kiss a little hotter than the one before until they were both damn near panting.

A horn sounded behind him, and lights flickered, and he dragged himself back to focus on the road. "You're addictive," he muttered.

"I'm still not sure what's going on," she confessed, "but I like it."

Gage moved his hand to grasp hers, linking them on top of her thigh. "We're almost to your house. We'll talk there."

Because he wanted to be looking her in the eye when he made his next move.

That plan wasn't as simple to execute as he'd hoped, now that they'd let their attraction out of the bag. He parked and pulled her out the door after him, and they ended up kissing, grinding together against the outside of his truck before he realized where they were.

Out in public. In her driveway. Within spitting distance, or at least seeing distance, of where her father still lived in rooms above the garage shop.

Gage tugged her to the front door and she attempted to unlock it. Only there was this spot on the back of her neck that screamed for him to kiss it, and the next thing he knew he had his lips on her skin, his arms around her, and she was moaning in this sexy way that made his knees shake.

"Oh *God*, Gage, I can't think when you do that." A full-body shiver rocked her as the door finally swung open, and if he wasn't careful, he was going to have her pinned to the wall in less than thirty seconds.

And while he couldn't remember why, that would be a bad thing.

KATY WAS past the "what is going on?" stage and was well into the "whatever is going on, it better not be a dream" stage. She abandoned her purse to the floor and the next thing she knew her fingers were tangled in Gage's hair, her tongue in his mouth. The front door slammed shut—had to be Gage kicking it, because she'd had nothing on her mind except getting close to him all over again.

The passion raging through her body was unfamiliar, and she didn't ever want it to stop. Didn't want *him* to stop.

He dragged his lips down her neck, hands scrambling to push her coat from her shoulders. She fumbled with his shirt, tugging it free from his jeans so she could press her bare hands against his naked chest.

Heat. Like fire licking over her, hot desire raced up her back. "God, Gage, what are we doing?" She hated to whisper the words. The last thing she wanted to do was to interrupt this, whatever *this* was, but she had to know.

He stilled himself, her hands on his tight abs, his fingers poised over the buttons on her shirt. "You want me to stop?"

"No, but what is this? A one-night-stand? Or..." Damn, she remembered something important. "You're leaving tomorrow."

His eyes flashed, and he nodded, dragging a finger over her cheek. "And you're not seeing Simon anymore."

A light bulb went off in her head. "Oh."

A sheepish smile transformed his expression from sex god to reluctant, yet adorable, boy next door. "I couldn't very well ask you to go out with me when you were seeing him, but now I'm leaving for six months, and maybe it's crazy, but..."

"You want me to go out with you? Like, see each other exclusively?"

The instant response visible on his face was even clearer than his words. "Hell, yes."

She stroked back the lock of hair that had fallen across his forehead. "Okay."

Gage grinned for a moment then it faded. "I have to

leave tomorrow, Katy. I made the commitment, and I need the money to—"

A slip of the hand moved her fingers over his lips to stem the flood of words. "I know you have to go. It's okay. You'll be back in six months, which kind of sucks to wait for a second date, but I can live with it. What I want to know is what we're doing *tonight.*"

"You're incredible." Gage shook his head. "And I'm a shit for making a move now, but I've been watching you for ages, woman. I couldn't risk waiting any longer."

He couldn't have been watching and waiting as long as she had. "It's not a big deal. I need a break after dating jackass Simon anyway."

Gage's eyes darkened, and not in a good way. "Did he hurt you?"

She shrugged, sliding her hands around to his back and easing their bodies closer. She wanted to get back to what they'd been doing. "Does it matter?"

"Yes." Gage tucked his fingers under her chin and lifted. "What's wrong? What did he do to you?"

Katy sighed, the aching desire in her limbs still there, but fading. She wished she could stare at her feet while she admitted this, but instead she picked a spot over his shoulder. Pretended he wasn't really there. Whispered her confession. "He'd started to get pretty bossy about a lot of things, and I didn't like it. Plus, he didn't think I was very good in bed. Not adventurous enough, or something."

If curses had burst from his lips, she would have nodded in understanding. If he'd hummed knowingly before patting her shoulder in sympathy, it would have made sense as well.

Him busting out laughing was the last thing she'd expected. It wasn't laughing *at* her, though. Didn't make her uncomfortable, just sent another zing of lust up her spine, over her shoulders and zipping back down between her legs.

Gage dipped his head until their eyes were on the same level, his amusement fading as the fires turned back to desire. "Any guy who thinks you suck in the sack—it's his damn fault, not yours."

She wiggled. "You say that, but... I mean, how could you know?"

He drew a line down the placket of her shirt, playing his fingertips over the buttons like an erotic connect-the-dots. The heel of his hand barely brushed the swell of her breast, and her breath hitched. "You're walking sex, Katy. You make me hard by just breathing. We've done nothing more than kiss, and I already know you're going to blow my mind."

She wanted to blow more than that, but her cheeks had flushed to feverish temperatures. "Thanks."

"Don't thank me," he warned as his gaze dropped down her body, his finger circling the button on her jeans. "I'm too damn ready to prove it. Right here. Right now."

There was this uneasy itch between her shoulders. Katy wanted harder than she ever remembered wanting, and with that deadline hanging over their heads?

She wasn't sure where she pulled the confidence from but, thank the Lord, poise she didn't usually feel arrived. "Do it."

Gage's head whipped up. "Do...what?"

Katy lifted her hands to her buttons and popped the first one open. "Do me. Here, and now."

The entire time she worked on her shirt he didn't move, except for the heavy breathing. Her every move was examined closely, though, his lids dropping to hide his eyes. She shrugged the material off her shoulders and allowed it to puddle on the floor.

His throat moved as he swallowed. Whispered, "Say it's not crazy. Say this is what you want, even though I'm leaving tomorrow."

"I want you," Katy confessed. "And it's not crazy—not completely." She reached behind her and unhooked her bra. "I'm tired of sitting back and being told what's going to happen in my life. I want this, Gage. I want *you*, even more because you're leaving soon. There is no tomorrow, so give me today."

Her bra joined her shirt on the floor, and that was it. Discussion over.

Gage had her in his arms, her feet dangling in the air as he carried her down the hall to her bedroom. Their lips connected, the worn fabric of his T-shirt soft against her naked chest. He paused to toe off his boots, and they bounced off a few walls en route. Her legs were wrapped around his hips, her hands traveling over his shoulders and back as she savoured finally getting to touch him.

The thought of the last occasion she'd been with her now-ex blipped in and out of her brain, taking barely a moment. About as long as the actual act had taken, if she was honest. She'd certainly gotten no pleasure from it, not like the incredible sensations rocking her body this time around.

Gage lowered her to the bed and stepped back. He reached over his head to grab his T-shirt, jerking it forward and off his muscular torso. His biceps flexed, chest muscles and chiseled abs clearly visible in the light streaming through the window. She admired the dark dusting of hair on his chest, another dark trail leading down into the jeans that were even now being unbuttoned, unzipped and frantically cast to the floor.

"Get naked," Gage ordered. "I want skin, and nothing but skin tonight. I want enough touching to make me crazy for the next months while I think back to tonight."

She wiggled off her jeans and undies, staring at him in awe. "I'd ask for a picture, but your image is branded on my brain. You're gorgeous, Gage."

He crawled onto the foot of the bed, tossing her clothing on top of his. "I'll send you a picture from my cell phone."

"A dirty one?" she dared to ask.

"No, not dirty." Gage dropped a condom on the pillow, and her heart did this funny thump. With his knees on either side of her body, he had her trapped. Elbows to the sides of her torso, and a slow, deliberate connection between them followed as he settled on top of her. "You want naked from me, you only get it in real life. But I'll email you..."

He kissed her. Soft again, like in the parking lot.

Another retreat, and another steamy grin. "...I'll send you texts..."

Gage traced the edge of her jaw to her neck, kissing his way up to the sensitive spot under her ear.

"...I'll be back in late March, and we'll make that our New Year's celebration. I'll prove exactly how much I'll have missed you. And exactly how perfect we are together."

"Gage, *oh*..."

He'd stopped talking and started, well, everything else. Kisses and caresses, his lips on her torso as his fingers plumped her breast. His tongue tracing circles around her nipple a second before his lips closed over the tip and he sucked. A sharp, aching need shot from his mouth to directly between her legs, and Katy could no more hold back her groans than fly to the moon.

It wasn't just one thing, it was the complete seduction. His hands on her stomach, sneaking over her belly to tease the folds of her sex. His mouth doing sinfully good things to her breasts. Katy's heart pounded, her body growing slick as he teased her, fingers on her clit, fingers slipping inside her.

"I'm going to make you come, and this first time? I'm going to watch."

Gage hung over her, his face only inches away as his hand worked her, a rapid thrust of his fingers driving her toward a peak faster than expected. His pupils dilated further as she groaned his name, her nails digging into his broad shoulders.

He kissed her breathless then vanished, sliding down her body like a human tornado. More caresses, long slow strokes—he avoided her sex for a moment, and she was glad until the continued touches made her twitch with the desire.

"Hmm, delicious." Gage opened her legs with his shoulders and dropped to tease her folds with his tongue. Gentle at first, then bolder until she was arching up to his mouth, grinding against him as he thrust his tongue deep. As he covered her sensitive clit and sucked, flicking the tip with his tongue until she broke into a million pieces.

She turned into a puddle on the mattress, barely able to focus. He snatched up the condom and covered himself, lowering over her to touch their heated foreheads together.

Gage breathed out slowly as his cock nudged her core. "You ready for me?"

Years ago. Forever. All the words she wanted to say she held back, instead simply nodding.

He slid inside, and she shook, fighting to keep her eyes open so she could add the expression on his face to the whole experience. Bliss mixed with the hunger, and a moan escaped him as she crossed her heels against his lower back. The change of position slipped him deeper so they were all-the-way connected.

Skin to skin, fully engaged as they stared into each other's eyes. Gage pulled his hips back, and pressure skittered past sensitive nerve endings, making her entire body heat further.

He thrust forward, and again, catching hold of her hip to lift her higher. He pinned her in position as the pressure and tempo increased.

"Sweet Katy. Oh my *God*, so bloody good." Gage tilted his hips at the end of each thrust, and she gasped. "Okay?" he asked.

"Oh, this is..." She couldn't breathe to get the words out, but she didn't want him to stop. "Yes, good. *So* good."

He kissed her, his breath hot on her cheek before he tangled their tongues, thrusting into her mouth in imitation of his cock.

Katy saw lights sparkling before her eyes when they broke apart to gasp for air. "I'm close. Oh, Gage, how? How can this...?"

"You feel it, Katy? How good we fit? How fucking good we are together?" He pressed her to the mattress and grabbed both her thighs, looming over her and opening her in a whole new way. The changed angle increased the tension, and when he slipped his fingers over her clit, she was lost.

"*Gage...*" Katy shouted his name. She clutched her thighs as he drove in one final time, his cock held deep while her body convulsed around him.

Stars floated past her vision as he shook, his body gone taut—his abdomen, his chest, all the lovely muscles under her exploring fingers.

She closed her eyes, and everything reduced to sensations. To the touch of his lips to her cheek, the added heat as he rolled them to the side. Gage hitched her leg over his waist, rocking his hips gently as his hard-on continued to stretch her.

Katy opened her eyes to discover his sexy smile waiting for her. That one lock of hair was back over his forehead, and she brushed it away tenderly.

"Hey." Her cheeks flushed with heat.

Gage traced his fingers over her shoulder. "Hey. That was..." His sigh screamed of satisfaction as he met her gaze. "Trust me, you're nothing short of mind-meltingly sexy, and I want to do that at least a couple more times tonight."

"Deal." Katy buried her face against him, suddenly shy. What if...

His lips touched the top of her head. "Thank you."

Her wavering doubts faded. She lifted her chin. "You don't think I was too forward? That we did this too soon?"

Gage stroked her cheek with his knuckles, his expression gone serious. "Katy, we've known each other for years. We've cared about each other since we were teens. It's the next step, and yeah, maybe it's fast in some ways, but it makes sense. Far more than any one-night stand or mere physical attraction." He tilted her head. "You wanted this, right?"

She nodded.

His smile stole out. "Then don't doubt it. Accept it. If I could, I'd be here tomorrow night, and the night after that, but since I can't, we'll take tonight as the start. I'll warn you, I want more. More than just incredible mind-numbing sex."

A shiver took her as he withdrew and left an empty spot in her body, like his leaving would create an empty spot in her heart. "I'm going to miss you, Gage. You've been around forever."

"...and you really know how to shake my tree. Go on, you can say it," he teased.

Katy laughed, rolling on top of his naked body before slipping off to allow him to deal with the condom. "What does that even mean?" she asked.

"Hell if I know." Gage rejoined her on the bed. "Now, come here. I have a couple more condoms. If we nap in-between, I figure we can use them, and I'll still get enough rest for the trip."

Katy curled up naked next to him. Gage slipped an arm over her stomach, and tucked her as close as possible. His strong arm held her, his beautiful body warmed her, and a slow trickle of renewed excitement grew from the contact. "Gage?"

He breathed slowly, contentment in his tone as they relaxed. "Yeah, Katy?"

"That was a very memorable start to this..." She paused.

"Relationship," he said firmly. He kissed the back of her neck. "You're mine, I'm yours, albeit from seven hundred kilometres apart for a while. It'll work out. You'll see."

The happy glow in her heart matched the satisfied lethargy in her limbs, and she closed her eyes for a few minutes to rest until he woke her up and started all over again.

And again.

All night long. Incredible, satisfying. Life was damn near perfect.

CHAPTER 3

When the alarm on Gage's watch went off early in the morning, Katy found it was harder to keep happy thoughts at the front of her brain.

Had she thought this was perfect? Far from it. She pulled herself to vertical, leaning against the pillows to watch as Gage dressed quickly so he could leave.

He slipped back onto the edge of the bed and pulled her into his arms, kissing her passionately. "I'll be in touch. I promise. And time will pass quick enough, okay?"

She nodded, swaying from side to side uneasily. "You want me to tell Clay we're dating?"

"Would you?" Gage grinned. "Nah, I'm kidding. I'll call him." He shook his finger in her face. "Don't let him give you hell."

"Clay?" She pretended to not be worried. "He's a pussycat."

Gage laughed loudly before giving her one last tender kiss.

She crawled out of bed and followed him to the door,

standing on the porch to watch him drive away. The dark, cloud-filled sky reflected her internal mood. What a night. Incredible.

Except for the part where he'd had to leave.

Katy stepped inside and gave up on bed, pulling on her clothes and staring through the kitchen window at the grey fall day. It wasn't fair that he was gone this soon...

Foolish inspiration hit. He'd said he was still packing a few things this morning. She could at least go and visit while he worked. Or if he needed to concentrate, she'd just sit.

After how many years of not being together, and a guaranteed six months' hiatus in the future, why not grab every single moment they could now?

She'd drive over to his place and...

...and her car was in the shop. Frack.

Fine. She could deal with that. Katy laughed at the craziness of her actions, but they somehow fit the craziness of the preceding night.

She popped on her bicycle and did the short trip to the garage in record time, the grey clouds overhead not encouraging, but the lightness in her heart giving her limbs extra strength.

It wasn't necessary. She could email him, but something about wanting to see him one last time called to her. One more chance to make it clear that she was happy they were together, that this was a bump in the road.

She let herself into the garage and grabbed her key from the TO BE SERVICED hooks on the wall. Threw up the overhead door and rolled out quietly. There was no reason to disturb her dad because she knew she'd get a lecture about driving past her scheduled service mileage. *Older vehicles like yours need to be kept well maintained, yada, yada, yada...*

She'd deal with her father's pet peeve once she was home.

Now? She had to get to Gage's place before he left. One more kiss. One more kiss would make it all worthwhile.

She wasn't even to the highway when the threatening rain became a full-fledged downpour. She clicked the wipers to high for all the good it did, the heavy moisture streaming upward across the windshield creating a waterfall in reverse as she took the car up to barely highway speeds. The turn approached for the gravel road that would take her to Gage's place, and she applied the brakes.

Nothing happened.

She tapped them again, increasing pressure as the turn not only approached but flew past her, the upcoming curve racing nearer far too quickly.

"Oh, shit." Katy jammed into a lower gear to slow the vehicle's momentum, but it didn't help. Rain glistened on the road's surface, long ribbons of water like miniature rivers and...

Her wheels hydroplaned. The car shimmied to the side and hit the ditch, bouncing violently as the tires crushed the tall, uncut grass.

Katy jerked forward slightly before her seat belt locked, choking tight across her chest. Fear screamed through her veins as she fought with the wheel, steering toward an open space in the trees. Everything rushed past as if she weren't seeing the entire picture.

Trees.

Road.

Water.

Grey sky.

The screaming of the engine, the smell of wet brake pads.

Then pain as the car bounced, the single airbag in the steering wheel *whooshed* to full, and her head slammed into the doorframe.

CHAPTER 4

To: Katybug@gmail.com
04:07:00 Sunday, September 13

Made it to Fort Mac. That was a hell of a drive at the start. The storm didn't ease off until I was past Edmonton. Held me up enough I didn't get in until after midnight, so I didn't want to call and wake you up.

I've got good news and bad news.

The company that hired me had a screaming good offer waiting when I arrived. It's a shorter contract, at nearly double the pay. The catch is we're going remote. No time off, no Internet for the entire two months. They're flying us into the bush, and I'll be welding for up to twenty hours a day. Fun, right? Sucks in a way, but means I'll be back sooner. And I want to be back sooner.

I'll be gone by the time you get this message. Leaving early

hours Sunday. Take care of yourself, and kick Clay for me.
j/k

Don't let that asshole Simon jerk you around anymore,
beautiful.

I miss you already. I can't wait to get back so I can date you
properly. Getting to share Friday night with you was a dream
come true, but as hot as the sex was? I want more for us. I
mean it. This is something I've wanted—you're something
I've wanted—for a long time.

GageJ@hotmail.com

p.s. I love that you used your nickname for an email address

Gage wondered about including that part about wanting so much more than sex, but at the same time it was what he'd been thinking the entire drive north. What he'd considered first thing after being offered the crazy increased tempo job.

Anything that got him back sooner was a good thing, even though no communication at all was going to make the time apart rougher.

Two months wasn't long, though, not in the big scheme of things. And when he got back? They could start up where they'd left off, and head into better and better territory.

He prepared to deal with the second impossible message of his morning.

"Five minutes," the coordinator warned, grabbing Gage's duffle bag and loading it onto a trolley. "Chopper pilot wants to get out ahead of the storm."

"No problem." Gage rose to his feet and followed the man toward the airstrip where his transport waited. "Last message."

Only it was a problem. Explaining that he and Katy were dating was like walking into a minefield. He didn't know if Clay would be upset about Gage hooking up with his sister, but disappearing into the north right afterward was sure to rub the lot of the Thompson boys wrong. Desperation hit. Gage opened his email and checked the note he'd composed the night before.

Hey, Clay

Since Katy had the sense to break up with that ass Simon, I figured it was a good time to stop any other jerks from stepping in and making a play for her.

Katy and I had a good long talk Friday night...

Right. *Talk.* Talking with their hands. And heated kisses. And naked bodies...and if he let his mind continue on this path he'd be walking to the chopper with a hard-on.

...and we both thought it would be cool if we were an item.

Gage cringed. It sounded as lame now as it had the night before.

It sucks that I'm gone for a while, but it can't be helped. I sent Katy a message about my change of plans. When I get home in November, I intend on doing everything possible to make her happy. Can you keep the wolves at bay while I'm gone? Your sister is a damn special woman, and I mean to make sure she knows that.

"Time, buddy. Let's roll."

Shit. "Okay, okay." Gage hit send and hoped it would be enough for now.

It had to be enough. He shoved his phone into his pocket and shouldered his carry-on bag. Walked into the cold north wind and the unknown. Left behind his heart and his future.

Just a little while, Katy, just a little while.

CHAPTER 5

November, Rocky Mountain House

Katy slapped her palm against the door to her small house, slamming it shut behind her.

The door reopened not two seconds later. "Will you stop running away from me?" Janey demanded. "I asked a question."

"I don't know the answer, okay? And it's pissing me off," Katy snapped.

"Oh." Janey sighed, kicking off her boots before easing herself onto the back of the couch. She planted her feet on the seat cushion and nodded sadly. "Another of your memory gaps?"

Katy glared over her shoulder as she draped her jacket on a wall coat hook. "Memory gaps. Such small words for such a huge, bloody nuisance."

"Hey, stop being so rough on yourself. The doctors said things should come back. Sometime."

Sometime was another not very reassuring word. Katy

stomped across the room to stand with folded arms, glaring at her friend. "Janey, I still haven't figured out the passwords to my computer. You had to help me pay my bills so my power didn't get cut off. I'm relearning how to do the data entry at the garage, which means I'm basically a freeloader with my own family."

"They don't mind. None of us mind." Janey shook her head. "Please, stop beating yourself up. Stop acting as if, since your car wasn't totaled, you don't have the right to be injured. A few obstacles are worth dealing with until you're back up to speed."

Obstacles. *Fah.* Another word that was as bad as *memory gaps*.

Katy clomped into the kitchen and whipped open the fridge, but just like the past couple of weeks, nothing looked even remotely appetizing. Her stomach churned. "To answer the next question I know you're going to ask, no, I'm not going tonight."

"Another answer I don't understand." Janey bounded off the couch and came over to hang on the fridge door. "It's Gage. You remember this part. He's the guy you've been mooning over for years. You really don't want to be there when he gets home from Fort Mac?"

"No," Katy lied. She sniffed the milk in the carton before pushing it at Janey. "Does this smell okay to you?"

Janey rolled her eyes. "Don't think I don't know what you're doing, because I *know*. I'm your best friend, dude, and the chances of you pulling bullshit on me—zilch. Zero. Zippo."

She examined the milk carefully, wrinkling her nose before she nodded approval.

Katy caved a little. "Okay, you're right. I'm lying. I want

to see Gage, but I'm fighting off that stupid flu bug that's going around. Add in I think the whole idea of a surprise party is stupid, and I don't want anything to do with it. If I'd been out of town for a couple months and had driven nearly seven hours to get home, the last thing I'd want to find at the other end is a house full of people and noise."

Her friend shrugged. "Your brother set it up."

"Doesn't make it any less stupid of an idea," Katy pointed out, taking the milk back and replacing it on the shelf. "In fact, it makes it even more important I not go. Clay was listed as Gage's emergency contact—that's the only reason he found out Gage was coming home early. Who's to say whatever is bringing Gage home four months early is good news? If something bad happened, it's not like Gage will want a party. And the last thing I need is for Gage to be pissed off at me before I try to make some changes. He'll never see me as anything more than Clay's little sister if I'm always tagging along like I did when we were younger."

She gave up on the idea of food and wandered back into the living room, Janey hard on her heels.

"You plan on making a move on him, then?" Janey asked.

"Eventually." Katy threw herself on the couch and stared at the ceiling. "I'll let him settle in first. Maybe I'll ask him to dance, or something, next Friday at Traders. You know, start small."

Janey towered over her, a frown creasing her forehead as she tapped her foot on the hardwood floor. "Maybe I should do the same with Len. Your brother is the most frustrating man I've ever met. I mean, I all but offered myself up on a silver platter to him once..."

Katy raised both brows in disbelief.

A guilty snort escaped Janey. "Okay, *more* than once, but you know, every single time he's turned me down." Her eyes widened to huge circles for a second, then her lashes fluttered like some regency heroine. "What if it's hopeless? Maybe Len isn't attracted to me. Oh dear, what if he's sick of me being around, and he's been humouring me all this time? What if I never get to experience those hunkalicious arms wrapped around me, or feel his beefy body pressed firmly against mine?"

Katy laughed at the obvious melodrama. "First, no one talks like that. And second, you're nauseating me. I get that you like my brother, but ick on the sexy talk about him. I don't need to know that stuff."

"You mean I can't share detailed accounts of our wild nights of debauchery with you?"

Even as Katy laughed, her stomach rolled again. "No. Once you get debauched, you're on your own."

Janey settled on the coffee table, and her laughing smile faded slightly. "Okay, I'll stop teasing. If you're not up for the party, we'll make sure we track Gage down some other time."

"Now we sound like big-game hunters or something. 'Don't shoot until you can spot the blue in their eyes.' I don't know that two against one is sporting."

"Screw sporting. We want what we want, and we both deserve great guys." Janey leaned forward and squeezed Katy's knee. "Seriously for a minute, you're still my best friend. No matter what changes you're going through since the accident. I have to keep telling myself that while you look exactly the same, you're different."

"That's encouraging." Katy pulled a face. "I think."

Janey blew a raspberry. "Oh come on, you know what I mean. You're still my friend, Katy, but you are changing, and I wanted to make sure you knew I like the new you as much as the old one. Remember *that*, okay?"

The sweet, caring smile on her friend's face meant as much as the words did. "Thanks, Janey. I'm glad I've got you. Makes the changes a little less scary." Gravel crunched outside, and she and Janey twisted to face the windows. The familiar pickup truck idling in her driveway did little to settle Katy's stomach. "Damn."

"Freak boy," Janey muttered. "What the hell does he want?"

Katy intercepted the door before Janey could reach it. "I don't care what he wants, he's not getting it, not until I figure out what *I* want. But you have to promise me not to go off the deep end, or you can get your butt out the back-door now."

"Simon's an ass."

Katy snorted. "Yes, so you've told me, but you still can't hit him."

Janey sighed lustily. "Fine. I'll stand way over here and will only kick his balls to Saskatchewan if he does something stupid. Deal?"

Overprotective, but Katy loved her friend for it. She wiggled her fingers and waited until Janey had taken a few steps away like she'd promised. "Be good."

"Good as gold."

Katy faced the door and waited for the knock that had to be coming. Seeing the doorknob twist first only increased her exasperation with her boyfriend—ex-boyfriend. Only confirmed what Janey had told her regarding Simon's inappropriate behaviour.

She undid the deadbolt and jerked the door into the

room in time to catch Simon with his hand raised, knuckles toward the wood.

He blinked in surprise then smiled. "Hey, girl. Looking good."

"What do you want?" Small talk was out. Long discussions were out. Any involvement with the man was out. Not until she actually remembered what their situation was.

Sheer sadness crossed his face. "Now, sugar, don't be like that. I take it you still don't remember us. You've got to let me take care of you, hon. You're so on your own here, and you don't have to be."

Out of the corner of her eye Katy spotted Janey stepping into view. "I'm not on my own, but thanks. You're right, I still don't remember."

"Asshole. She broke up with you—"

Katy lifted a hand to stop Janey's outburst. "Don't you start."

"But he—"

"Don't," Katy snapped.

Janey crossed her arms and glared daggers at Simon.

He shuffled slightly. "I wanted to make sure you were doing okay. See if there's anything I can do."

"I'm fine," Katy insisted, the tug of unease at the back of her brain only increasing.

She knew she'd been going out with him. Janey and other people, including her brothers, had insisted they'd broken up. Simon insisted just as strongly that they had gotten back together the night before her accident.

The lack of certainty was making her crazy. Crazier.

It wasn't as if they had to be together now even if they had been before, but Katy had to admit feeling a touch of sympathy for the guy if he was telling the truth.

Sympathy didn't mean she was going to kiss him or automatically let him back into her life.

Simon looked her over slowly, sorrow deepening in his dark eyes. "If you need help, you be sure to let me know. I miss you, sugar."

Janey made a vomiting noise in the background, and Katy schooled her expression to stop from smiling. "Thanks, Simon. But I really am fine."

"You let me know if you think of anything. Or if you remember more, or if you just need to talk." Simon caught her hand before she could step back. He lifted her fingers to his mouth and kissed them tenderly. "I'm here for you."

Nothing. No response to his touch and kiss. Well, nothing more than that constant roll of nausea that now might be caused from not eating all afternoon.

She extracted her hand and got Simon to leave with only one more rude comment from Janey.

Her friend plopped her fists on her hips and stared out the window as Simon backed out of the driveway. "Good riddance."

"I like how you were so well behaved," Katy deadpanned.

Janey waved farewell at the retreating back of Simon's truck with her middle finger raised. "I was brilliant, wasn't I?"

Laughter swelled up, and Katy let it free, hugging her friend before seeing Janey out the door with a promise to get together the next day.

There might be holes in her memory, and lingering frustrations, but there were a lot of good things in her life. Between Janey and her family, somehow she'd get through this rough patch, and make it out the other side.

Of course, thirty seconds later she was running to the

bathroom to throw up, which erased a good portion of her optimism. It was tough to stay positive while bowing in front of the porcelain throne.

HE HADN'T EXACTLY SPED the whole way home. Gage was sure there were a few sections of highway where he'd briefly slowed to the speed limit. When there were too many cars for him to dodge.

Since the plane dropped him off at six a.m., he'd been going nonstop. Pretty much like he'd been going for the previous two months. Working like a madman before falling exhausted into bed for a few hours to get up and do it all over again.

The good part was the blistering pace kept him from obsessing about Katy before falling asleep. It did nothing to stop the dirty dreams that invaded his brain and had him waking with more than simple morning wood.

With a very short stop for a shower and a nice paycheque in his pocket, he'd crawled into his car and hit the road. Even the two-month growth of beard he left unshaved, because it would take too long to deal with.

He wanted to see Katy.

Driving with one hand, he used the other to check his mail. There were a mess of texts and emails in his inbox, most of it spam, but none from her. The message he'd sent to Clay moments before leaving had bounced back as well with a *Message undeliverable. Recipient's mailbox is full. Fatal daemon error.*

Curses drifted through his brain. He punched in Katy's number only to have the phone die on him, the battery dead. Fine. It was more important to be there and do the next thing in person anyway.

Like sweep Katy up in his arms and kiss her senseless.

The entire drive he daydreamed about where he'd find her. Timing-wise she should be at home, so he ignored his own place, and the garage, and took the back loop. The sight of her car in the drive made his heart leap, and he parked in the second snow-free space in a rush, damn near leaping from the truck. Somehow he forced his feet to a walk instead of rushing her front door and bursting in like a maniac.

He rang the doorbell.

Knocked.

Rang again.

It might be rude, but he even leaned over and peered in the window, to see if she was around. A pair of winter boots lay haphazardly under the hall coat rack, a small puddle of water pooled under the soles. Her coat was there—only no sign of her.

He moved to knock a second time but was interrupted by Katy's less-than-ladylike cussing. Gage tried the front door, and it opened easily.

"Katy? You here?" Both feet still on the outside stoop, he stuck his head around the doorframe to make himself heard.

A new set of sounds greeted him, less amusing than the curses. Retching and coughing, and Gage couldn't stand it any longer. He stormed forward and headed toward the bathroom.

"Katybug, you okay?"

She was seated on the floor, her cheek resting on one arm as she basically clung to the toilet. Her eyes were closed, and her face twisted in a grimace as she shuddered then leaned forward and spat.

"Oh hell, you got a stomach bug?"

Or that's what Gage intended to say. He got out the *Oh hell* part before Katy's eyes flew open and her gaze landed on him, all traces of nausea and exhaustion vanishing as she opened her mouth and screamed. She scrambled to her feet, hands flailing, a riot of noise and motion.

Damn. He held out a hand toward her. "Katy, hey, it's okay. It's me, Gage."

He ducked away from the toilet plunger she'd swung like a sword. At the same time he examined her quickly— noting her pale skin. The dark shadows under her eyes.

The business end of the plunger wavered in front of him as he took in her extremely short-cropped hair, the dark strands that usually would have covered her shoulders only about an inch long over her entire head. It was a radical change from before. Kinda cute, really, but unexpected.

"Gage?" She squinted, her head tilting to the side and making her rather adorable. Well, adorable if she weren't still threatening him with a toilet cleaner.

He took hold of the handle and tugged the shaft from her fingers, putting the weapon back in its place. "Yes, Gage."

"I don't remember this at all," she muttered. "You're not you."

He laughed, then caught her as she swayed. "And you must be running a fever or something."

She squirmed out of his arms and backed away slowly. "No fever. My stomach's upset. Feels better now." She looked him up and down quickly. "You're missing your surprise party."

Utter dread joined the disappointment in his gut. That

was the last thing he wanted tonight. "Don't tell me there are people over at my house."

Katy nodded then gestured toward the bathroom door. "Umm, if you don't mind. I need to brush my teeth. And stuff."

Of course she did. "You sure you feel okay?"

"Yeah." She waved him out, frowning as if confused.

His beard must be worse than he imagined.

"I'll wait in the living room." He thought about stealing a hug, but the last time he'd been in her shoes no way would he have wanted to get up close and personal with anyone right after throwing up.

He headed back to the living room, pausing to remove his boots and wipe up the snow he'd tracked in during his mad rush to help her. That's when he noticed there were other changes in her house since September. A lot more stuff for one thing. Fabric and paintbrushes in the hall, a stack of clothes draped over a chair in the kitchen beside a sewing machine. He had to move aside a pile of what looked like jigsaw puzzle pieces before he could sit on the couch.

It was as if a whirlwind had hit—it wasn't the spotless, nearly OCD-organized place he'd visited over the years.

Gage rose to his feet as she approached a few minutes later. "Better?"

She waved away his concern. "Fine. Just a touch off for a few days."

He couldn't wait any longer, closing the distance between them. If she was sick, that eliminated a too-personal welcome home, but that was okay. They'd leapt in at the start. Now he could go a little slower. Care for her. Take his time to make sure they had a solid foundation. He caressed the peach-fuzz softness just above her ear, stroking gently. "I like your hair."

Katy touched her head self-consciously. "It's okay. It's grown a lot since the accident."

The bottom fell out of his stomach. "Accident? What accident?"

She snorted before jerking to a stop, the golden flecks in her dark brown eyes flashing at him in the light. "You're serious. You didn't know I went into the ditch?"

He grabbed her hands tight. "I had no idea. I emailed you from Fort Mac before I went into the bush, and I haven't heard a thing since then. What happened?"

Katy stared at their joined hands, her mouth hanging slightly open. "Umm, Gage. It's okay. I mean it happened two months ago."

Her unease increased, and her body grew stiffer. Instead of curling up against him like he'd hoped, she withdrew, and the whole situation grew more awkward by the minute.

When she pulled her hands free, he let her go. Let her increase the distance between them. He attempted to focus on the other issue at hand. "You hit the ditch. Everything okay?" A snatch of memory struck him. "I thought your car was in the shop."

She pulled a face. "I guess that checkup was overdue. The brakes weren't good, or that's what they told me. The accident is a complete blur, though, so I'm not sure."

Gage glanced out the window. "Your car looks fine."

"Small mercies. No damage to it, other than the brakes. They told me I did a good job of driving her down the embankment. Never lost control or spun out—they could tell that from the tire tracks or something."

She was leaning on the wall opposite him now, a good five feet between them. Gage felt wrapped in cotton. "So...

how do we get from your great ditch driving to your hair being cut off?"

Katy took an enormous breath and let it out slowly. "They told me I bumped my head. Hard enough they shaved my hair off so they could attach test thingies. After a week's testing when nothing showed up on their machines, they told me I was fine."

Gage was the one frowning now, his entire body tensing as he slipped the clues together. "You keep saying 'they told me'. You don't remember the accident?"

She shook her head, frustration obviously rising. "I don't remember the accident, plus there are a few other gaps. I lost a ton of long-term memory as it relates to math—passwords, formulas and things like that. So it's nice you sent me an email, but I never got it. I had to set up a new email account because I couldn't get into the old one."

His jaw had to be hanging open, and his feet were pinned in place now, hands dangling uselessly by his sides.

Katy had lost her memory?

Had she forgotten *them*? If so, she'd have forgotten what they'd done. What they'd planned.

It would explain so much in terms of her discomfort with him—more than only nerves at having him back around after a long break.

He forced himself to speak even though his mouth had gone totally dry. "So...this amnesia. How extensive is it?"

Katy shrugged. "A couple weeks before the bump are fuzzy or gone—I'm not sure now what are real memories and what are things I've been told."

"A couple..."

It was true. In one swoop their future was rearranged. He wasn't about to pick her up caveman-like and tell her that *they* were another thing she'd forgotten. Not when she was still fighting frustration along with whatever else had her at less than one hundred percent physical health at the moment.

He also had no intention of letting her get away. The dilemma of how to move forward threw him into a tailspin.

As out of control as a car skidding into a ditch.

CHAPTER 6

K aty couldn't look away. The mustache and thick beard covering his lower jaw were part of it—the only thing familiar on Gage at first had been his eyes. Even they seemed slightly different, though, as she'd never seen him stare back at her with quite that expression before.

The one that said he was a split second away from swooping in to protect her. Which she might have liked the idea of in principle, but right now, no way.

After two months of having people walk on eggshells around her, she did not need another babysitter. Especially not Gage. Her own big brothers were more than enough of a pain in the patootie. Having the guy who turned her insides to sexual jelly acting all sympathetic and concerned—

Nope. She wanted him looking at her with a grown-up expression, not as if she were delicate china. Even if currently she was concentrating very hard to stay vertical and not dash back to the bathroom.

Stupid stomach flu.

Another wave of dizziness struck. "Gage—this is fun

and all, but I need to call it a night. You've got people at your place, and I want to crash."

Gage blinked before straightening, the entire solid package of male shifting awkwardly toward the door. Like he was hesitating between reaching for her or following her request.

He made a noise. A deep and grumbly complaint kind of like a possessive bear, and if she'd felt a smidgen better, it would have made her toes curl with delight.

She slipped past him and caught the doorknob, swinging the door open so she could use the solid frame as an anchor to keep herself vertical.

"Okay. I'll go." He paused. "You need anything?"

Katy clutched the door harder. "Twenty-four hours' shuteye, but thanks for asking."

Gage paced forward reluctantly. "I hope you're feeling better soon."

"Thanks. And have fun at your party."

She lasted until he was in his truck before she locked the door and raced for the bathroom. Classy. Elegant. Way to impress the guy. She couldn't muster the strength to feel embarrassed. Crawling into bed after she'd rinsed her mouth was the only thing on her mind.

Although the feverish dreams she had that night of Gage Jenick doing dirty things to her were a lovely distraction.

Two mornings later the flu was still hanging on, though the nausea was no longer a 24/7 thing. With the fresh taste of toothpaste lingering on her tongue, Katy strolled into her living room.

Janey had taken up residence on the couch, feet propped on the coffee table. "Sick again?" she asked.

"Duh." Katy lowered herself gingerly into a chair.

"You're the master of the obvious today. Stupid flu bug will not let go of me."

A pale pink box flew across the room, and Katy caught it instinctively.

"If I'm the Queen of Obvious, then you're my lady in waiting. Flu, *shmuu*."

Katy twisted the box toward her, reading out loud. "*First Hint. The early pregnancy detection*— Hokey spit, Janey."

"If the morning sickness fits..."

Protests at this point were futile, but there were other more important issues. "Please tell me you didn't buy this at the local Safeway."

"You think I'm stupid?" Janey folded her arms across her chest. "I was in Red Deer yesterday. No one we know anywhere around, and yes, I looked. Now go pee on the stick so I can tell you *I told you so*."

The whole idea was stupid. Impossible.

But...

The twinge of doubt at the back of her brain was enough to tip Katy into caving. "Stay here," she ordered. "I don't need supervision."

Janey ignored her, leaping off the couch and following her down the hall. "I went through the directions a couple times. I'll help."

"I have to pee on something," Katy drawled. "It's not rocket science."

Her friend had already opened the box and pulled out what looked like a small stir stick. She held it forward. "Have a ball."

Janey retreated enough to give Katy a moment's privacy, but Katy had to admit it was kind of nice to have her there as they stared at the stick lying on the counter.

"If that thing let off a bang about now, I bet we'd both scream loud enough they'd hear us in Calgary," Janey quipped.

Katy looked away for a moment to brace herself. If it was positive, what then?

Pregnant. On top of everything else?

"How could I be pregnant, Janey? You told me I wasn't with Simon for a while."

Her friend wrinkled her nose. "If it wasn't Simon, then who? You got hit by an influx of midi-chlorians or something?"

Janey held the stick in the air, the two pink positive lines clear and bold. Undeniable.

"Fuck." Katy leaned on the bathroom door, working to calm her breathing. "Okay, I can deal with this. It's not the end of the world. It's..."

Bursting into tears was the last thing she'd intended, but it happened. A moment later she was being supported by Janey's firm hug. Petted and coddled all over again like her brothers had been doing for the past two months, but this time she wanted the pampering. At least for a few minutes.

When she pulled herself together, Janey handed her a fresh wad of tissue to replace the set she'd ravaged.

Katy wiped up the last of her tears. "Thanks for being a brat and bringing me the test."

Janey nodded. "What you going to do, girl? You don't have to keep it, you know. Especially not knowing..."

"Not knowing who the dad is?" Katy's stomach fell three feet as she considered Simon might be the father. Her memories of him in some areas were clear enough to know he'd been trouble near the end of their relationship. What *she* considered the end. Did she really want to raise a baby with him around? "I have to sleep on it. Give it more thought. I'm not rushing into anything, not right off."

Janey gave her a look. "Fine. I won't push, but whatever you decide, I'm here for you, okay?"

Katy hugged her. "Thanks."

They shuffled awkwardly for a moment before Janey sighed. "Not much use hanging out here unless you want me to try to break into your passwords on the computer again."

"That's not important right now. I have other things to worry about." Katy groaned. "And now that I know why I'm sick, I guess I'll find some ways to feel better."

"Rest. More vitamins." Janey nodded. "I'll do some research."

"Careful. I don't want anyone to know until..."

Until time allowed the information to truly soak in. They nodded at each other, jokes and kidding put aside for once as this new secret they shared was beyond any childish prank or youthful daydream.

Janey left her with a final hug.

Secrets.

One great big secret that was only going to get bigger. Literally bigger.

Katy wandered into the kitchen to make herself a cup of tea while she considered. There was a person growing inside her. She tossed a piece of bread into the toaster, staring out the window as the timer clicked down, the noise echoing in the silent house.

A baby.

Click. Click. Click.

She'd told Janey she would think about it, but there was nothing to think about. She'd didn't want to have an abortion. And giving up her baby? Impossible.

It was clear. She was going to be a mom.

Now the mystery was...would there be a dad or not? That one wasn't nearly as cut and dried.

GAGE STARED AT THE HOUSE, wishing he'd done this right the first time, immediately after getting home. Six days was as long as he could wait before nearly going stir-crazy. He'd used the time to ask questions on the sly. To gather as much information as possible, so when he made a move it would be in her best interest and not simply following his gut response to take control.

To reassure himself all over again this was the right thing, him getting involved in her life.

It hadn't been a lack of bravery that had made him walk away from Katy that first night. It was trying to keep the possessive beast inside him under wraps. He'd worked so hard to be different than his father. To be considered patient, and caring. Gentle even.

Bubbling inside were far different emotions. Holding back was too much to ask, and he didn't want to wait any longer.

Katy needed to know what they'd done. What they'd agreed to. She'd had time since the accident. If their relationship ended up being another issue to deal with, at least they'd deal with it together. That didn't make him an asshole.

He knocked on the door, anxious to get started.

The woman who greeted him was still on the green side, and his heart went out to her even as his gaze took in the rounded curves under her housecoat.

"Oh, look. Gage Jenick. I barely recognized you without your beard."

She was cracking jokes. That was a good sign. "You still sick?"

She shrugged. "Feeling a bit better. What's up?"

Had to seem strange since he didn't usually drop in on her like this. Not before they'd...

"I need to talk to you."

Katy frowned. "Something wrong with my brothers? Or at the garage?"

"No, nothing. This is personal."

That only seemed to confuse her more. "Give me a second to pull on some clothes, okay?"

He paced the room until she returned, unable to settle in one spot. All the reasons he had gone slowly with establishing a relationship were valid ones—yet there didn't have to be roadblocks anymore. Part of him wanted to leap up and cheer. The other tightened the ropes he'd looped around himself years ago, ordering himself to maintain control.

Right now she needed a friend in her life, not another bossy male. Somehow he would find the strength to behave and not fuck this up.

"Want something to drink?" she offered.

He shook his head. "I needed to talk to you about your accident. More specifically, the night before."

Katy collapsed onto the couch. "This is old boring territory, Gage. I don't—"

"Humour me. I know it's boring because you've said it a million times, but I haven't heard it."

Katy the brat showed up, rolling her eyes at him before responding. "I was out for the night. Went home. Got my car the next morning, and went off the road into the ditch and bumped my head. You think book or movie options would sell better?"

He ignored the snark. "How did you get home from the bar?"

She opened her mouth, then closed it quickly. "Oh. You drove me. That's right, Clay told me that. Thanks, if I didn't say it before."

Damn it. Gage let a growl of frustration escape. "Katy. We weren't worried about our *please* and *thank-yous* when we got here that night."

Her eyes widened. "What are you talking about?"

He lowered himself beside her on the couch and slipped his hand over hers. "Something happened that night. We both wanted it, and if I hadn't gone north, we'd be together now."

Her entire body went rigid. "Together, as in how?"

Gage stroked her fingers gently, willing her to at least remember his touch. "We made love, Katy. A bunch of times. And it was hot and amazing, and I can't wait to do it again."

The pallor of her skin brightened as twin red spots flushed her cheeks. "We...made love. After you drove me home."

Her confusion was understandable, so he nodded and went on. "I know it was shitty timing, not only because of the accident, but because I had to leave the next day. I'm so sorry I wasn't here for you. Sorry you had to deal with your accident without me around, but I intend on being here for you from now on. No matter what you need."

"Oh, for fuck's sake." Katy jerked her hand from his and snapped to her feet. "Who told you? Did Janey tell you? I'm going to kill her."

Not the reaction he'd been looking for. "Tell me what? I haven't seen Janey."

"Right," she drawled. Her eyes narrowed. "Don't do this, Gage. The last thing I need on top of everything else is someone pretending they want to be with me out of a sense of obligation."

"What makes you think I feel obligated to be with you?" Gage rose as well, looking down at her small form that vibrated with anger. "Hell, Katy, I've been lusting after you for a long time, and that night was one of the best things that ever happened to me."

"Kind of like my family was the best thing ever? A safe place in the storm after all those foster families?" Katy stomped away a few feet before twirling on him. "Okay, that wasn't nice. I'm glad you feel like one of the family, Gage, but I certainly never thought you were the type to be willing to sacrifice your entire future on a whim like this."

Somewhere their wires had gotten crossed. "I have no idea how me being a foster kid, or your family, is even involved in this discussion, or what the hell sacrificing my future means. Before I left we said we would work on being together. On spending time and getting to know each other more."

"Sweet sentiment, especially when you toss in having a kid. Babies aren't something you can return to the store when they become inconvenient, Gage."

Wait. What?

"Babies? What are you talking about?"

She froze with her mouth open as panic slipped into her eyes.

A pit opened in front of Gage, and he stood with one foot in midair over the unfathomable depths. He took in all the signs, lined up the data, then waited for his ability to speak to return.

"Wait, are you telling me you're pregnant?"

Holy shit. Holy fuck. Holy crap.

Katy took a deep breath before muttering her response. "So. That went well."

"Answer the question." Gage narrowed the gap between them. "Are you serious? You're pregnant?"

She frowned. "You sure you didn't know?"

"How could I know? Oh man, Katy. I had no idea." Gage wasn't sure his feet would continue to hold him. It might be a cop-out, but the room was wavering. "I need to sit down."

He stumbled backward and collapsed onto the couch. Katy was pregnant. They'd had sex, she'd had an accident, and he...

They...

She...

Katy snickered. "You want me to get you some smelling salts?"

Gage lifted his gaze to meet hers. "How far along are you?"

It was her turn to pause. "Oh, shit, you're not serious, are you?"

"About what?"

Katy dropped into the seat opposite him. She made the most hysterical face as she scratched her head. "Good grief. Okay—for the sake of discussion, let's assume you're telling the truth. You drove me home and we spent the night knocking boots."

"It is true."

She glared at him. "Let me talk this through without interruption, or I will kick your ass out the door."

His head was still spinning from trying to process the idea of a baby on the way. "You've gotten an attitude since I left," he observed.

"Comes from being knocked around and knocked up." She stared at the ceiling before leaning forward and asking very earnestly. "Now if we did the horizontal mambo, was there a reason why I'd be pregnant? Did we not use a condom? Did it break?"

Gage shook his head. "We used protection, every time. Including in the shower."

Her cheeks went bright red at his comment, but she pushed forward. "Then it makes no sense. It couldn't be you. If...you know, we did what you said."

"It can happen. Condoms aren't foolproof, and we were pretty enthusiastic." His stomach was in knots. Gage paused. He wasn't trying to get out of his responsibilities, but it would be stupid not to get all the details. "You had the accident the day after I left. Not to be indelicate, but have you been with anyone since?"

She snorted. "Are you freaking kidding me? I've been lucky to go shopping without supervision. Clay and the boys have had me on lockdown ever since."

Gage nodded. "I can believe that. Okay, then. Mystery solved."

He dragged a hand through his hair, wondering if he should go hug her or kiss her, or do something other than sit like a bump on a log as he attempted to get over the shock.

Katy grimaced. "Um..."

He saw her, heard her, but his brain was racing a million miles an hour.

A baby.

Sweet mercy, he'd had one night with Katy, and they'd

gone and got her pregnant. There was so much wrong with that in so many ways he could barely put one thought behind another.

He wanted Katy. Wanted to care for her, and be there for her.

Being a father? Not on the list of things he had planned. Not today, maybe not ever.

"There is..." Katy crossed her arms and damn near rumbled with frustration. "Damn it. Damn it, *damn it*."

"What?"

"Okay, the only guy I *know* I had sex with, because while you say we did, I don't remember it, so sorry for this, but I did have sex with Simon. It could be he's the dad."

A wave of furious anger struck like a lightning bolt. Gage wasn't sure how he ended up on his feet towering over her, but the mere idea of Simon back in Katy's life was enough to tear down all his hesitations. "Not bloody likely."

She shrugged. "True facts, Gage. I had sex with him."

"You broke up with him." Gage caught her hands in his as he shoved his internal misgivings and fears into the corner. He didn't want to be an asshole, but no fucking way was she going to be with anyone but him. "We had our night, I sent you an email—"

"Which I never got," Katy pointed out. "Simon was here the other day, insisting that we'd gotten back together. How can I know for sure?"

"It doesn't matter," Gage insisted. "You don't want to be with him. You want to do the best thing for you, and that's not being with him, it's being with me."

Katy paused. "You mean I need to do the best thing for the baby, right?"

Gage swallowed hard. "Right. For the bab—" The word

stuck in his throat. *God.* A *baby*. He switched tack and pulled his phone from his pocket. "Look. I should have the message I wrote you in my sent box."

"Gage..."

He ignored her growing scowl and instead scrambled back in his files, only to swear in frustration.

"What?"

Gage looked up into a set of deep brown eyes marred by sleepless shadows under them. "My email automatically clears old messages after thirty days."

"Convenient." Katy sighed. "Look, I need to think about this more." She made a face. "Talk to Simon, I guess."

Time to think was good. Gage resisted glancing at his watch, because he didn't give a fuck it wasn't even noon. His *thinking time* was going to require a couple hard shots of liquor. "I'll call you this afternoon."

She shook her head. "Tomorrow."

Blast it all. Gage took advantage of his height and crowded her. "Look, I'll admit it. I'm more than a touch floored right now, but that doesn't change what's important. I care about you, and whether or not you believe me, I know there is a good possibility I'm the father of your baby. So we can think things through, and talk about them, but there is one thing I want to make clear right now. I will be in your life, Katy Thompson. I will be there to help you, and there is nothing you can say that will change my mind."

For the first time since their strange conversation had begun, a faint hint of a real smile teased her lips and the lines at the corners of her eyes softened. She laid a hand on his crossed arms. "Thank you."

He didn't remember leaving. Next thing he knew he was in his truck tearing down a quiet back road. The radio remained silent while the snow blanketing the fields rose and fell like an endless sea around him.

Katy Thompson was pregnant, and he was going to be a father.

The ice and cold outside had nothing on the icy fear threatening to wrap itself around his heart.

CHAPTER 7

K aty debated long and hard before making the call, but it had to be done. She did make sure Janey didn't know the details. Last thing she needed in the room with her while talking to Simon was a lit bomb with a short fuse.

It had snowed overnight, and outside a clean layer of the white stuff covered everything. Her car, the walkway, the long driveway leading back to the main road. Normally she would have pulled on her coat and scarf and been out there already, the fresh air and rising sunshine refreshing her. Her stomach, however, still demanded she do nothing more than sit by the window with a cup of tea.

This morning she would talk to Simon. This evening at their weekly family dinner, she'd face her brothers.

It was like some nightmare she couldn't quite wake up from. The only thing keeping her from flipping out completely was the knowledge she had a roof over her head for the long run. The house was hers, lock, stock and barrel, an inheritance from her mom, along with enough money to make being a single mom bearable until the kid was in school and she could work more full-time hours.

And... It wasn't right, but the other thing grounding her? The expression in Gage's eyes the other day—

So serious. So determined and solid in spite of his surprise about the baby.

What if he was simply trying to rescue her out of gratitude for the way he'd been accepted into her family? Something inside her wanted to say *So what?* Everything she knew about Gage said he was a good man, and if he wanted to throw in his lot with her and a baby for the next sixteen-plus years, she'd be crazy to turn him down. No matter how wrong it was to take advantage of his offer.

But first there was the issue of Simon.

Outside, a large truck with an attached snow blade was doing loops down her driveway. One of her brothers was taking care of the chore like usual, and she had to smile. They were good to her.

They were all going to freak tonight when she told them about the baby. But they'd freak, and then they'd buckle down and be there for her. Like always.

The doorbell rang, and she realized she'd been daydreaming in the sunshine. Time to face the music.

Simon beamed as she opened the door. "Hey, sugar. You're looking better. Beat that flu bug finally?"

"Sort of." She stepped back to let him enter, sidestepping his embrace. "Thanks for coming over."

"No prob." His smile tightened as Katy continued to evade his moves into her personal space. He finally gave up and turned to the living room, making himself comfortable on the couch. "I was glad to hear from you. I've missed you a ton. It's been hell since your accident."

He was telling her.

"There have been lots of changes lately. The accident, and a few other things have started to develop." There. That was a nice hint of foreshadowing. She was about to dive in when her phone rang—her dad. "Sorry, have to get this."

Simon waved her off, and she stepped into the kitchen to find some privacy.

"Hi, Dad."

"Don't you 'Hi Dad' me, little girl."

Shoot. Katy's tongue stuck to the roof of her mouth. Did he already know? "What?" she asked cautiously.

"You trying to pull a fast one on your old man, or what?"

Her amusement came out a little shaky. "Me pull something on you? You've mistaken me for one of the boys."

Keith Thompson barked out a laugh before getting to his point. "Hey, don't bother bringing anything for dinner tonight. It's all covered."

"Really?"

"Gage is back in town."

Yes, he was, but that didn't answer her question. "And this means dinner is set because...?"

"He called me."

Oh. Shit. "Really."

"You thought you could keep that a secret, didn't you? Nope—he called to say hello, and let me know he plans on being around more often. Good man, that one. Turned out well."

She wondered if her dad would change his opinion and whip out the clamps and tire irons once he heard the rest of the supposed story. "Dinner...?" she hinted.

"Right. He's bringing Chinese food. Him and Clay. Don't be late, or I won't be able to hold back the ravaging hordes otherwise known as your brothers."

Maybe full stomachs would make the news easier to hear. "I'll be there."

Well. That was going to add some excitement to the evening. Gage wanted to be there when she announced her pregnancy? She wasn't sure what she thought about that yet.

But first to deal with the issue of Simon.

Katy pushed through the door to the living room to find her self-declared boyfriend was no longer on the couch. She peeked around more thoroughly to discover his boots were gone, along with the coat he'd hung by the door. "Simon?"

She stepped up to the front window just in time to see his truck vanish down the driveway.

What the heck was that about?

Katy wavered between dismay and happiness that he was gone. She still hadn't told him about the baby, which only dragged things out even more. Postponing the madness wasn't the way to go.

That's when she noticed the papers she'd piled neatly on the coffee table were now scattered over the surface. The ones she'd printed out regarding what to expect during pregnancy, and her calculations on when the baby might arrive based on possible conception dates.

There were a lot of question marks on the pages, but Simon's name was clear enough.

Well, there was a part of her answer. He'd seen the information, put two and two together, and his first response was to run for the hills? Better to know now than later.

She leaned on the wall and practiced breathing out her frustration in time with the slow, steady scrapes of the shovel outside her door. Whoever had been clearing her driveway had switched to the front path and stairs, and the even rasps were strangely calming.

Eventually the noises stopped, and the doorbell rang. Katy expected to see one of her brothers, although they usually stormed in, no matter how often she asked them to knock. Instead it was Gage who leaned on the shovel he'd just finished using on the front stairs. Somehow he still managed to look all dangerous and sexy even considering the pink plastic handle.

He grinned. "Morning."

Katy glanced past him at the walkways. "Morning. You've been busy."

"No use in letting it pile up." He cleared his throat. "Can I come in?"

She opened the door and let him pass. "I hear you're joining us for dinner tonight."

He paused in the middle of unzipping his coat, guilty expression on full. "I was going to tell you that."

Katy fluttered her lashes at him in an exaggerated manner. "You fail at understanding the gossip chain. Dad must have called me within ten minutes of your offer."

He waited until he was facing her square on. "You're going to tell them tonight, aren't you?"

All her amusement slipped away. "Yes, and it would have been tough enough without having you there."

He shook his head. "It would be tougher to tell them without me. I'm involved, Katy, one hundred percent. You don't have to do this alone. None of it."

His words made something inside her gut ache, in a good way this time. "My dad was right—you're a good man, Gage Jenick. A good man with a death wish, but still."

He'd toed off his boots and followed her into the living

area. "It's not going to be easy, but I don't think the guys will outright kill me. Put me in traction, maybe."

They settled across from each other, his gaze staying firmly on her face. Katy ignored him best she could as she gathered the papers strewn on the table.

The silence stretched on for far too long.

"So..." Gage broke off then cleared his throat. "I hate that there's this wall between us. I'm not going to walk on eggshells anymore, so if I step over a line, tell me to go to hell, okay? We can stop this stupid awkwardness and be honest with each other."

"Fine by me." Katy leaned back and waited for whatever bomb he wanted to drop this time.

"What did Simon say?" Gage blurted out.

"Ha, is this why you gave me the *honesty* spiel? You spotted him leaving." Katy loosened her fingers from where she'd unintentionally clutched her thighs. "I think he's a little surprised and needs time to mull it over."

Gage glowered. "You're not sure?"

She pulled a face. "He kind of left as soon as he found out."

That made Gage pause, and he shifted positions uncomfortably. "Okay, moving forward then. While I hate the idea of involving him at all, what are your plans for the future?"

"In terms of...?" Katy wasn't sure what he was asking. "I'm keeping the baby, if that's what you mean."

He shook his head. "I meant in terms of Simon and me. I told you where I stand. I want to be there for you. If the baby is ours then it's far simpler than if Simon is the dad."

Katy sighed. "Simon doesn't seem very interested in being a dad, but I suppose I need to give him time. Not everyone is *rah-rah, baby, baby!* instantly." Not even her,

67

although she'd already come to love the kid in a surprisingly short amount of time.

"I looked online. There are tests we can do to find out which of us is the father." Gage's eyes were like magnets, trapping her under his gaze.

Of all the conversations she never expected to have. "I checked as well, but that's another issue I'm flipping back and forth on like a flag in a high wind."

"It would answer the question once and for all," Gage offered.

"It would, and with everything else I have no memory of, or control over, a solid answer would be nice..." A shudder shook her. "And then I start thinking about all the testing I went through after the accident, and I'm just so damn tired of being a pin cushion. One minute the peace of mind from knowing is worth it. The next, the risk involved for the baby, no matter how small, is too much to chance."

Across from her, Gage leaned forward, elbows resting on his knees. "You don't have to rush. You don't have to decide now, but—God, I can't believe I'm saying this—I'd prefer you to wait."

"Really?"

He sighed, long and hard, before nodding. "Katy, I've said it before that I'm ninety-nine percent sure this baby is ours. Waiting for confirmation will suck, but why do anything even remotely dangerous when waiting a little longer gives a safe answer? We can do the test after the kid is born."

"If we do that, nothing will be settled for sure until June," she warned.

"I can live with that."

Katy leaned back, examining her gut response to the idea now that there'd been another opinion voiced. Under the circumstances, it was her decision alone, but knowing that Gage wasn't pushing for an immediate answer made her butterflies of indecision settle. "Then we'll wait."

He didn't leap up and cheer or anything, but she could tell he was pleased. Having made a solid decision regarding the testing gave her a strange kind of peace.

She'd still have months of uncertainty, but it felt like the right thing to do. And with the way Simon had taken off like a shot, there might be a chance he wasn't going to be around at all.

"And until then...?" he asked.

She shrugged. "Until then life goes on as usual. I try to get over this stupid amnesia as it relates to numbers so I can go back to working at the garage. I take it you'll be starting up at the shop?"

Gage frowned. "I meant what about us?"

Oh boy.

"I..." *He wanted honesty.* Katy lifted her eyes to meet his square on. "I like you, Gage. Part of me really hopes what you're saying is true because I've wanted to get involved with you for a long time. Of course, that means if we did fool around and I've forgotten, I'm doubly pissed off, because I'd been waiting forever, and it's just wrong to have lost those memories."

His smile had widened, the sexy one that melted her butter faster than it should. "Trust me, I can hardly wait to make some new ones."

Dammit. Dammit. *Dammit.* She held up a hand as if to ward him off. "But we can't. Not yet."

Confusion crowded his expression. "If you want to be with me, and I want to be with you, then why aren't we getting together, Katy? Why aren't we facing the future, and your pregnancy, as partners the way we should?"

A wave of sadness and frustration rolled over her leaving her exhausted. "What if Simon is the dad?"

Gage all but growled. "First, I'm damn positive he's not, but more importantly, you don't want to be with him. You don't *have* to be with him just because he said you'd made up."

"And you said we fooled around, but I. Don't. Remember." Katy's voice rose higher as she spoke. She shot to her feet, her hands wrapped around a throw pillow that had been passed down from her Gramma, its fine decorative needlework spelling out *Bless This House*. She squeezed the fabric as she paced the room. "Give me a break. I admitted that I've always liked you, Gage, but as far as I know we've never even *kissed*. How on earth can I simply go 'hey, okay' and dive headfirst into a long-term relationship with you? None of it makes sense, and not being sure is frustrating me more and more."

Anger boiled over, and she whipped the pillow from her hands. It spun across the room, narrowly missing a table lamp. Katy pressed her fists against her temples as she fought to settle down.

Stupid hormones. Or maybe the "new Katy" had triggered her over-the-top response. The one with far too much vinegar in her blood.

Gage hadn't taken his gaze off her. Probably worried she'd flipped out, and might turn on him next, and do crazy things. She dragged a hand over the short mess of hair that had regrown and let out a frustrated grumble.

Gage was on his feet in an instant, gently rubbing her upper arms as he made soothing noises. He pulled her against his chest, and it wasn't sexual, just comfort and understanding.

Katy twisted her face to the side, slipped her arms

around him and accepted his hug. Let the warmth of the embrace twine around them. Let the smooth repetitive touch of his hands down her back relax away the tension. She stood there in his arms for a good five minutes before all the frustration and fire had eased off enough that she could finally take a deep breath.

Gage squeezed her a little tighter. "I'm here for you. Like this, if nothing more. My commitment has no agendas, no deadlines. Just one moment after another until we make it through."

Under her cheek his heart pumped out a smooth, even tempo, and Katy clung tight. To the firm support of his body and gentle touch of his hands. While she'd wanted him for a long time in some half-dreamed-of sexual-fantasy world, right now things were still so unsettled. Visions of Simon walking away, and the unknown reactions of her family during the evening ahead loomed over her...

It was nice to have one solid place to stand. One solid individual she could lean against who helped stop the spinning, even for a moment.

She stepped away from him reluctantly. As nice as it was to have his support, she wanted one thing clear. "Dinner."

"You have any requests other than your usual pineapple chicken balls?"

It should have been a good sign that her stomach didn't do a roller-coaster trip at the suggestion of greasy food. "Other than that. Promise me you'll let me tell them myself."

He scowled.

Oh, hell no. This was not up for debate. "I will tell them that you've been nothing but supportive. Just let me do it my way, okay, Gage? They're my family."

Disagreement hovered—she saw it in his eyes.

Such expressive eyes he had. She'd never noticed quite as much before as in the past couple days. Everything he felt was right there. No secrets for Gage. His emotions were worn on his sleeve.

But he finally nodded. Gathered his coat and headed out the door, and this time as she watched yet another truck depart down the snowy drive, it was with a faint sense of hope.

CHAPTER 8

Gage wondered what his chances were of making it through the evening without at least a black eye.

There were seven of them gathered tonight. Katy and himself. Mr. Thompson. The four boys started with Clay and rolled on down through Mitch, Len and Troy. Six years separated oldest from youngest, and all of them except Katy were over six feet.

They worked together. Played together, and basically tormented the hell out of each other like any true family. And they protected their own with a vengeance.

His getting Katy pregnant was not going to go over well.

Len nabbed a third helping from one of the takeout containers scattered over the table. "Even after I checked it thoroughly, Tanya Lynn insisted there was something 'funny' with her engine. I think it was a ploy to get Troy to take her for a test drive."

"Did you take her for a test drive?" Clay taunted his youngest brother. "I thought you'd done that a few times last month already."

73

"Fuck off." Troy didn't even blink. "You don't seem to mind dealing with the repeat business of checking Carrie Taylor's nearly brand-new Yukon."

"She rides it hard," Clay offered as an excuse.

"That's what I hear."

Gage laughed along with the rest of them. "You seeing Carrie Taylor, Clay? That's new since I've been gone."

Clay shrugged. "She's alright."

Troy directed a smirk at Mitch, obviously hoping to get attention off himself and onto someone else in the room. "Saw you got pulled over by Anna Coleman. Trying to set a new record for speeding tickets?"

Mitch leaned back, no denial on his face. "Not my fault she likes her men fast."

Mr. Thompson cut in. "Enough about your love lives. Lord, I'd swear you were all a bunch of old women the way you go on at times. Gage, I want to know what you've got planned for the next while now that you got the travel bug out of your system. You sticking around Rocky more permanently, or did you like it up north?"

Beside him Katy wiggled. She'd been awfully quiet for most of the meal. Partly because it was impossible to get a word in edgewise. Mostly, though, he suspected she was nervous about sharing her news.

He understood the sensation. There was a huge knot in his belly. "Definitely sticking around Rocky. I made nice coin during my stint, but the oil fields are no place to work full time."

The older man nodded. "You going to keep on at the shop with us then?"

"Yes, sir. No use in taking business from you—there's not enough work for two shops."

Talk turned to more business items for a bit. Familiar and easy, and Gage's mind drifted.

The massive round table they were gathered around had been one of the first places in Rocky Mountain House Gage had truly felt welcome. His foster parents had meant well, and they'd been the best of the lot he'd ever had, but a caring couple in their late sixties couldn't fill the holes in a fifteen-year-old's heart. Couldn't give the acceptance and real family feeling he'd gotten when Clay had brought him home to the Thompson dinner table.

Back then Meg Thompson had still been alive. She'd taken one look at Gage before hugging him tight then shoving fresh baking and an enormous list of chores on him and Clay.

The inclusion on the work list had meant more than the food and hugs. Belonging included sweat equity—Gage had known that instinctively.

He'd sat down at that first dinner with the four Thompson boys and ten-year-old Katy, and he'd felt at home for the first time since his own mother had been violently stolen from his life.

Beside him Katy had a definite case of ants in the pants, fidgeting like crazy until he wondered that none of the guys were noticing her strange behaviour. Gage laid a hand on her thigh out of sight of the others. Casual-like. Just a light pressure to let her know he was there for her.

Her entire body tightened, and she darted a glance around the table to see if anyone was watching.

Everyone else was far too interested in their conversation and their plates to spot anything. He leaned over slightly to whisper by her ear. "You know they love you to pieces. It's going to be just fine, Katybug."

His use of her nickname made her lips twitch. But even more importantly, to his delight she snuck her hand over his, linking their fingers together and squeezing tightly in response.

The sudden silence alerted him. All attention had turned their direction. Food and drink forgotten as five sets of dark eyes bore into him and Katy.

"You two got something on your mind over there?" Clay's question buzzed angrily in Gage's ears.

It was rather amazing how much disapproval could be put into such simple words.

Katy took a deep breath, but before she could speak Gage decided what the hell. He'd sooner be skinned for the whole disaster, no matter what she'd said before.

"Not a secret," Gage announced. "We're dating."

Other than her quick gasp of shock, there was no response to his comment. Not for a full five seconds. Then an uproar of noise hit from all sides.

"The hell?"

"Since when?"

"Are you serious?"

Over all the questions and cussing lay a deep, heavy rumble, starting low then increasing in volume until Mr. Thompson's laugh broke through. He waved his sons off.

"Calm yourself, boys. You really surprised by this?" He clicked his tongue. "Never thought I'd raised a pack of dullards. I saw this coming from a mile away."

Katy gave Gage a dirty look before facing her father. "What's that mean?"

The older man shrugged. "Means I'd seen you two making calf eyes at each other when you thought no one was looking. About time you came to your senses."

Clay stumbled to vertical, glaring daggers at Gage. "Bullshit. You can't be dating Katy."

Gage stood to meet him eye to eye across the table. "Not your decision."

"She's still recovering from the accident. She doesn't need to get involved with anyone."

A stream of very creative swearing burst free from a most unexpected source. Gage waited cautiously until Clay looked away before also turning toward Katy.

She'd stood as well, her much shorter status very clear as everyone loomed over her from where they'd all risen to their feet around the table. The vile language spewing from her mouth stuttered to a stop as she whipped out her finger and stuck it in her oldest brother's face.

"The accident happened two months ago. I. Bumped. My. Head. That's it. I didn't have a lobotomy or revert to childhood. I've had enough of you wrapping me in cotton and refusing to let me do anything on my own. Yes, I have gaps in my memory, and yes, dealing with that is a pain in the ass. But you, Clay"—she glared around the table to take in all her brothers—"*all* of you, are even bigger pains. I did not break my brain, or my body. My sex drive did not vanish out the broken window, and I will not allow you, or anyone else, decide what will or won't happen in my life."

Gage wasn't sure the mention of sex was the wisest idea as eyes narrowed further, and fists were clenched. Only he couldn't worry about that because she'd spun her fury toward him.

"And you! You're the biggest pain of them all. I told you I wanted to do this myself. You agreed, and now you just leap in and do exactly the opposite of what I asked for? Damn you." Katy stepped back from the table, her eyes full of fire as she planted her feet wide and crossed her arms. "Gage and I are *not* going out," she stated clearly.

Oh, shit. She was more upset by his taking control than

he'd expected. He reached for her, but she twisted from his grasp.

"Forget it, Gage. We might be seeing more of each other in the future if you get your head out of your ass, but the only reason will be because you might be the father of my baby."

"*What?*"

The question exploded from five male throats at the same moment.

Katy lifted her chin, cheeks red, her chest heaving. "Yes. I'm pregnant. No, I'm not sure who the father is, although Gage insists he could be. It's either him or Simon, and that's all I'm going to say about this tonight because I'm sick of all of you. Good night."

She twirled on her heel and stomped from the room, the door slamming shut after her. Gage wavered between running after her and staying to explain to the guys.

He never saw it coming. The fist that connected with his jaw made stars burst before his eyes, and he stumbled backward before landing on the floor, five very angry faces staring down at him.

"Shall we bury him alive in the back forty?" Mitch asked, wiggling his fingers to shake out the blow he'd delivered.

"Hang him in the garage. We can use the welder's torch and skin him first."

Gage shoved aside the anger inside that wanted to flare like a torch. "Let me explain, dammit."

Clay dragged a hand over his head then gestured his brothers aside. He extended his hand to Gage.

Gage eyed it with distrust.

His friend snorted. "Look, you surprised us all, but I'm

not going to beat you any further, and neither will the others."

"Speak for yourself," Len drawled. "What the hell is going on, Gage?"

"Boys, let him up." Keith Thompson pushed through his sons to cast an unreadable stare upon Gage.

Gage accepted his friend's help and was dragged to his feet. His hand rose instinctively to his face to cup his stinging jaw. "I can explain."

He gave the best short version he could. All the while their disapproval weighed down on him.

"Dammit, Gage." Clay paced away. "And now you've gone and put her back up. Idiot."

"Thanks for telling me something I didn't know."

Len looked disappointed. "Does this mean we're not killing him and hiding the body?"

Mitch rested a hand on his shoulder. "Not today, but there's still hope for tomorrow."

And with that, Gage sighed in relief. He was going to be forgiven, at least by the guys. Katy, on the other hand, was another issue. He'd have to watch his balls around her for the next while.

They all settled around the table, a little uneasy. More awkward than he'd ever felt with the family.

"So, now what?" Len asked.

"That one is easy," Keith Thompson answered. "Now Gage finds a way to convince Katy they're a couple. If she's going to have a baby, she needs all the support she can get."

"So you'd better find a way to convince Katy she wants you in her life, or else," Clay snapped.

Clay's ultimatum pissed Gage off all over.

"There's nothing I want more." The secret seed of fear inside was shoved down and ignored as Gage went nose to nose with his stubborn best friend. "Did you not listen to what I said about sending you an email, you stupid ass? Did you not hear the part about how I'm the one who came to her before she even told me about the baby?"

"Easy words to say when none of it can be proved."

"Still say we take him outside and work him over," Len muttered.

"Shut up, all of you." Mr. Thompson didn't shout. Didn't storm, but his intensely spoken comment quelled all four of his sons. "Stop poking at Gage. He knows what he did was wrong, and if my baby girl is going to have a man in her life, I like Gage a hell of a lot more than Simon."

Warmth rushed him at the man's words of acceptance. "Thank you, sir."

Keith turned toward him with ice in the depths of his grey eyes. "You hurt her again, though, and I'll shoot you myself."

Ahh, family. Gage straightened up and wondered if he was going to survive.

Remembering the expression of fury in Katy's eyes, he just might be better off dealing with the guys.

CHAPTER 9

"**Y**ou want a baby shower before or after the kid is born?"

Katy pulled herself alert. She was only a moment away from sliding into a puddle of relaxation in the overstuffed easy chair, tired from her week and everything that had been going on. "There's a choice?"

Janey had plopped herself on the floor to apply a new layer of polish to Katy's toes. "Sure. I have two cousins, and one did it one way, and one did it the other. It's really up to you."

Tamara Coleman laughed. "How about both? Any reason to party is a good one."

Outside the snowdrifts were growing in height daily, but inside the room was warm, music playing softly in the background. Finger foods covered the table. Pitchers of both alcoholic and nonalcoholic drinks stood at the ready as the six women sprawled comfortably, relaxing after a long workweek.

Instead of Friday night at the pub, Janey had suggested

a girls' home spa. The laid-back evening was so much better than fighting the noise and the crowds. Katy was in heaven.

Lisa Coleman, who had been one of Katy's classmates in school, examined her sparkly nails critically. "It's easier to buy stuff after the baby is born, but then you also tend to get a ton of all blue or all pink outfits."

"Skipping away from the baby talk for a minute." Tamara leaned forward on her elbows. "Tell me to butt out if you're not sharing, but what's this I hear about Gage Jenick basically camping out in your front yard?"

Katy wasn't sure if she was pissed off or pleased with his relentless attention. "I laid down the law about two weeks ago, and ever since he's been trying to get back in my good books."

"Is it working?"

Janey snorted. "Gage has not yet perfected the art of the grovel, we'll just put it that way."

"Hmm." Shannon and Liz, two more of Katy's friends, exchanged glances. "A good grovel is always nice," Shannon admitted.

"Followed by make-up sex, right?" Liz grinned. "So, what's he not doing right? Not being determined enough?"

Katy stopped to think for a minute. Gage had been persistent—that much was in his favour. "I don't think he understands what he did wrong in the first place."

"Of course he doesn't." Tamara grabbed a pitcher and topped up her drink. "He's a guy. The words 'I was wrong' kind of stick in their throats and end up coming out as 'Get over it, little woman, I know best.'"

A snort escaped before Katy could stop it. "Yeah, that's about the entire story."

"So, all he needs to do is say he was wrong?" Janey tilted

her head to the side. "I would have thought this situation required more than that."

"Oh, 'I was wrong' would be the first step," Katy agreed. "But until he figures out that this is my life, I'm not letting him back in. It's bad enough with my brothers wanting to make decisions for me."

"And you don't need another big brother, right?" Lisa winked at her. "I know you probably hate getting asked, but how are you feeling?"

"Much better," Katy admitted happily. "Morning sickness is done. Lots of energy. I haven't got back my memory, but I have progressed in my math beyond two plus two is four."

"Hmm, too bad you have no memory of sexing it up with Gage." Shannon waggled her brows. "I bet he's got some moves."

"I bet he's not the only one out of the guys at the garage with moves." Janey's heavy sigh of frustration set the entire room laughing. "What?"

"Len turn you down again?" Liz asked.

Janey pouted. "This isn't supposed to be about me, but yes. Damn stupid sex-on-a-stick stubborn ass. I wonder if he's getting some on the side that helps him hold out against my charms?"

"Mrs. Palmer and her five sisters," Liz drawled.

Janey guffawed noisily, and things kind of went downhill for a while after that. Katy listened to the dirt talk and smiled as her girlfriends went to town about the guys they'd been seeing, or hadn't been seeing lately.

The Coleman sisters grinned at each other. "So basically no one in this room has gotten any action lately, except Katy, who can't remember how hot it was."

"Shut up." Teasingly said as Katy offered a smile. "This

is the Immaculate Conception over here, and don't you forget it."

"I can't believe sex with Gage wasn't memorable enough to stay in your brain no matter what. I mean, do you think he's got a teeny penis or something, and your mind is trying to wipe that out?"

"Not the size of the equipment, it's how well they use it," Liz quipped innocently, batting her lashes at the laughter that rose from the other women. "Well, that's what they say, right?"

"Who says? The guys with little dicks?" Tamara shook her head. "No, I doubt Gage is lacking penis power. Unless he's shoving socks into his jock strap, the guy's got the goods."

Like a barometer, Katy's cheeks had responded to the chatter. She didn't really want to speculate on Gage's... equipment. "Sorry. Memory loss doesn't pick and choose to save the juicier tidbits for repeat consumption. We'll have to stick with 'I don't remember' on this one."

"You know who has a tiny dick," Shannon muttered, staring into her third margarita.

Liz poked her. "Who?"

Shannon blinked then looked pointedly across the room. "Tamara's on-and-off-again beau from the hospital."

"Right." Tamara rolled her eyes. "Where did you hear that?"

"From you." Shannon smiled evilly. "You sent me an email with a bunch of forwards on it, and one of the old messages mentioned Dr. Tom should look into a penis enhancer."

"Oh shit." Tamara dropped her head into her hands while the room exploded with laughter. "Please tell me you deleted it."

"It's the Internet," Shannon groaned like a zombie. "It's forever. It will come back to haunt you..."

Tamara winced, then glanced around the room conspiratorially. "He does have a tiny dick."

Laughter exploded, and Katy relaxed back into her happy haze of food and friends.

It wasn't the size of Gage's equipment that interested her—well, okay, not completely. But if she remembered the act, she'd know for sure who was involved in making the baby in her belly. She slipped her hands over the slight bulge beginning to show and wished again for a miracle, like total recall.

It didn't come, but the friendship and warmth around her helped. Helped a lot.

OUTSIDE OF THE house and around the corner, Gage leaned on the wall. Tucked out of sight, he was bundled from head to toe in his thickest winter gear. The walkie-talkie he held to his ear alternatively answered his questions and made him blush.

Damn. And he'd thought guys talked shit.

A light buzzing sound registered in time for him to pull the speaker farther from his ear and not be deafened.

"You there, Gage?" Janey whispered.

He clicked on the speaker button. "Yeah."

"You hear what Katy wants from you?"

He couldn't resist. "Before or after she finds out the size of my package?"

Janey snorted then muffled her laughter. "Stop that. I'm in the bathroom. I'm going to turn off the walkie-talkie now if you have enough intel to get things straightened out between you and Katy."

"I think I do." A real apology. He could do that. "Thank you for setting this up for me."

"Hey, Katy does like you. A lot. But you pissed her off so hard. Don't do it again."

"I'll try not to." He resisted laughing. Being called up on the carpet by Janey was like being lectured to by a small, self-contained whirlwind.

"Don't fuck with me, Gage." Janey's voice tightened. "I went out on a limb for you here because I think you and Katy would be good together. But if you hurt her, I'll hunt you down and give you pain. Worse pain than the Thompson boys would ever dream of."

What was it with everyone in his life threatening him when he already wanted to do the right thing? "I just want to be there for her," Gage insisted.

"You better. Now go away. I want to drink some more."

"Thanks, Janey." He grinned as he stared into the distance. "If you ever need the same favour with Len, you let me know."

"Fuck off," she sang sweetly. "I can arrange my own seduction without your help."

He turned off the power and snuck away, careful to stick to the shadows and not let the girls discover he'd been eavesdropping.

Only putting what he'd learned into action was a hell of a lot harder than he'd expected. Yes, he'd known he'd fucked up, but he had apologized already.

Obviously it hadn't been sincere enough.

The next morning he shifted uneasily on his feet and waited for Katy to answer his knock. It was just past ten. Late enough she would have had time to sleep in a little and dress, because he didn't need any temptation to mess this up.

It sort of worked. She was awake. The woman who pulled the door open had bright eyes and a rested face; only she was still wrapped in a mass of soft terrycloth. Her robe ended at mid-thigh, and Gage snapped his gaze back up to safer territory.

He swallowed hard. "Hi."

She lifted one brow in a perfect Vulcan imitation. "Hi."

Gage paused. "How you doing?"

Katy nodded. "Good."

Ah, fuck it. "I'm so sorry, Katy. I was an ass, and I had no right to butt in and go around your wishes."

The door wavered a little as she hung on it, rocking slightly. "Go on."

Go on? Wasn't that enough? Gage struggled for more. Oh, his brilliant idea. He lifted the toolbox in his hand. "I can fix things."

Katy snorted and opened the door to allow him in. "You still need a coffee, don't you?"

There was no smell of caffeine on the air. "You're not drinking coffee right now, are you?"

She padded toward the kitchen. "No."

Gage made a flash decision. "Then neither am I."

Katy turned slowly to face him, her expression one of disbelief. "Why would you do that?"

He lowered the toolbox to the floor and followed her into the kitchen. "Because you love coffee, and if you have to give it up, I should too. As support for you while you're pregnant."

Katy rolled her eyes at him. "You can drink it, Gage. It's not going to kill me to have to smell coffee."

He shook his head. "Nope. I want to do this. To..." He

scrambled for words. "To experience a little of what you're going through."

"You want to go through delivery as well?" she asked dryly.

"Hell no." Gage grinned as he reached for the fridge door. "I'm not *that* brave."

There were tons of fruit and veggies and juice before him, so he poured himself a glass and offered Katy one.

She watched with a bemused attitude from where she'd pushed herself up to sit on the counter. "What are you doing, Gage?"

"Apologizing." He lifted his glass to her. "Trying to find a way to truly be there for you and make up for my stupid move at dinner a while back."

She tipped her glass toward him and they both drank deeply. Katy put her glass beside her on the counter and glanced toward the front hall. "You brought tools."

"Yeah." Gage leaned a hip on the counter beside her. "Wanted to have them around in case there was anything I could help with."

She shook her head. "Nothing broken. Nothing leaking or stuck. Sorry. Thanks for the offer, but I'm good."

Her feet kicked lightly as she watched him, her gaze lingering on his hands. Gage moved cautiously, afraid to spook her. "Okay. But have you thought about anything you need changed to get ready for the baby?"

She nodded slowly. "Yeah, I've been thinking about it."

He gazed out the window. "Maybe there's something there I could help with. If you'd like. Up to you, though."

God, this beating around the bush was going to kill him.

Katy didn't say anything for a while. Then this strange noise escaped her, and he whirled in a panic to check her. "Katy, you okay?"

Her shoulders were heaving. Heavy motion rocked her body, and he worried for a moment she was having some kind of seizure. Then she tossed her head back, and an enormous laugh burst free, echoing off the walls of the kitchen and driving into his soul.

Katy laughing was one of the things he'd come to treasure over the years.

Laughing at him? Not so much. "What?"

It took her a while to settle down, and she hiccupped a few times as she wiped tears from her eyes. "Oh God, Gage, this isn't you. So earnest and willing and...a total pushover. What the hell are you doing?"

What the heck? "I thought you wanted me to apologize."

She nodded, then shook her head. "I did, and I don't. I mean you were so out of line after I'd asked you not to interfere." She lifted her hand to touch his jaw where the final tinge of a bruise was slowly fading. "You got worked over by my brothers that night. I'm sorry for leaving you to them."

Gage stood stock-still as her soft fingers caressed his cheek. "I blew it more ways than one that night."

"You did." She patted his cheek gently then leaned forward to whisper, "But I'm ready to forgive you. Only for heaven's sake, stop acting like some ball-less dweeb."

Gage was the one to laugh this time. "That's blunt."

Katy shrugged. "It's the new Katy—I tend to speak my mind a little sooner. So here's the deal. You will not fuck up and go against my express wishes, and I'll stop my brothers from beating on you."

Gage nodded. "And you'll let me get involved in your life, however it will help you the most. Whether that's getting things ready for the baby's arrival, or being there to rub your feet or..." He'd spotted the circle on the calendar on the wall. "Or going to prenatal visits with you."

She hesitated. "I don't know how I feel about that."

"That's not true." Gage laid a hand over hers where it rested on the counter. "Come on, new Katy, tell me what's racing through your mind."

She stared down at their fingers. "I'm afraid to let you in, then find out you're not the dad, but Simon is. I'm afraid to have you around and then have you take off down the road." Her head lifted and those beautiful eyes stared into his soul. "I want you to be there for more than just the baby."

Gage stroked her fingers lightly. "I'm here. In spite of your fears." *In spite of his own.* "I wanted you before the baby was in the picture, and I'll want you no matter what." That much he could say with full and complete honesty.

The moment hung between them. Anticipation and longing right there. All his concerns and worries were overwhelmed by the need to have Katy make the decision *for him.* To be with him, and give him a chance.

Even though her accepting him would open up a world of nightmares—facing those would be worth it. Had to be worth it. He'd chosen to be a better man than his father, and this was the place that he made his stand.

Katy moved so slowly, but finally she did move. Leaned toward him and rested her head on his shoulder. He slipped up a hand to brush the inch-long hair over her scalp, the softness against his palm like satin.

She leaned away. "Okay."

His heart raced like an out-of-control train. "Okay?"

She nodded. "You can come to the prenatal with me. And you can do some stuff around here, to help get things ready for the baby."

Gage waited, then got tired of waiting. "And us?" he demanded.

Her tongue snuck out quickly as she moistened her lips. "Well, I suppose we could start seeing each other."

He wanted to toss his fist into the air and shout, but that might freak her out. So instead he picked her up and twirled her. Hugging her close as she laughed.

"Put me down, silly."

Gage lowered her carefully, reluctant to allow her warm, soft body to leave contact with his. "Does that mean we can go on a date?"

"Yes." She got an evil look in her eyes. "It also means I'm going to make you keep your promise."

He paused. "Which one?"

Katy slipped out the kitchen door. "No coffee."

Damn. "Not a problem."

"And don't think you can cheat," Katy warned as she found a spot on the couch and curled up. "I'm going to tell the boys, and Janey, and once I tell Janey *everyone* in Rocky will know. You try sneaking up to the window at Tim Hortons, and before you can say 'double double with a pack of Timbits', I'll be on your ass."

He lowered himself onto the open space next to her, leaving room between them. There would be time to make a move on the physical side of things soon enough, now that she was letting him in.

Letting him have a chance to do the right thing, and more. "No cheating, I promise. Now you want to tell me what you're thinking about for the baby?"

She leaned back, the sunshine in the window making her soft and edible, and incredibly beautiful. "You have any plans for the day?"

"You are my plans."

Her smile bloomed, and Gage's heart swelled a little.

It wasn't what he'd expected to be doing, talking baby rooms, but in the big scheme of things—it was right.

Except for that itch between his shoulders that poked him every now and then as Katy shared. And the ache in his gut that said he was a fool.

Gage ignored all the voices taunting him and focused on Katy. Focused on the future he wanted more than anything, even as his past sent out warning signs and threatened to break him.

CHAPTER 10

She still wasn't a hundred percent sure it was the right thing, but damn if having Gage Jenick shower attention on her wasn't a huge turn-on.

He'd hung around all day Saturday. Done every single thing she'd even glanced at in terms of cleanup or repair around the house—or at least what he could do without buying more materials than what he'd brought along in the back of his truck.

There was a new list on her fridge labeled *To Buy*, the sight of it a little unsettling.

"I can't afford too much, too soon," she warned. The idea he'd had to build a closet organizer for the baby's things was a good one, though. It would free up floor space in the tiny room. She considered her budget and how far she could tweak it before it screamed in protest.

Gage sat back on his heels, the hammer in his hand abandoned on the floor. "I don't mind buying stuff."

A rumble of discontent struck. "You're doing it again."

"Am not." He folded his arms across his chest.

A snort of amusement escaped her. "How can you deny it when you don't even know what I'm talking about yet?"

"From your expression, you're about to give me grief, and I know I haven't done anything wrong in the last five minutes."

His logic made her smile. Katy's butt was firmly planted where he'd pointed her at the start of their session. He'd carried her mom's old rocking chair from the porch into the baby's room. The worn wood under her fingers like a touchstone as she stroked it. "You can't go spending money I don't have."

"I'm not." The grin he shot her was far too cocky and adorable. "I'm spending my money, that I do have, to fix up the baby's room."

"Gage..."

He rose to his feet and snuck next to her chair. Trapping her wrists under his fingers, he moved in close. "Do you have any idea how much I earned per hour up north?"

The words whispered past her ears. Nearly as intoxicating as the heat of his breath caressing her cheek as he leaned over her.

Katy met his gaze—determined not to look away. "Doesn't matter. I still don't want you spending lots of money. It makes me uncomfortable."

They hung there for a moment, nearly close enough to touch. One small rock was all it would take to have their lips meet. Katy held herself completely immobile to avoid being the one to make the first move.

When he straightened, relief and disappointment wrestled for top billing.

Gage nodded, a slow dip of his head. "I can respect that, but there's a difference between me feeling obligated to spend money I don't have, and being pleased to spend money I do. So let me know what you feel comfortable with, and I'll try not to push you too far, too fast."

He tweaked her nose then dropped back into position to carry on fixing the floorboards.

His arm moved in a smooth rhythm, biceps flexing as the hammer fell with repetitive ease. The temperatures outside her little house had fallen below freezing, but the first thing Gage had done that morning was restock the wood pile and get the woodstove blazing.

The heat in the room—Katy wasn't sure if it was the fire or her crazy hormones.

Damn, the man was easy on the eyes.

"I'm going to make some supper." She paused in the doorway, glancing back in time to see him jerk his gaze off her butt and toward the floor. "You are staying for supper, right?"

He whipped out the dangerous smile. "I've got no plans to head anywhere else."

She paced down the hallway, a trickle of happiness rising. For a moment there, she'd thought he was going to kiss her. Maybe later tonight.

Now that the nausea was gone, her libido was working overtime.

Dinner was half from the freezer, half fresh cooked, and by the time she'd put the completed pot of spaghetti and reheated sauce on the counter, Gage had joined her in the kitchen.

He breathed in deep. "Heavenly."

"Twofer cooking." She pointed at the open cupboard, and he grabbed down plates. "Janey and the girls and I started it years ago. We cook up double batches and freeze the second serving, then we switch them around. Means we get to try new meals, but don't have to fuss with cutting back recipes for one person or end up eating the same meal too often."

"So you trade? Smart move." He loaded his plate then glanced around. "Table?"

Katy hesitated. She wanted something a little less formal even though it broke every rule she'd been raised with. "Want to watch a movie while we eat?"

Gage's eyes widened. "Katy Thompson, you heathen."

She hip-checked him lightly. "I know. Don't tell my dad."

He pressed a finger to his lips briefly, then tilted his head toward the couch. "Sit, and I'll bring the drinks."

Warm fire in the stove. Warm food in her belly.

Katy was going to blame the heat enveloping her on those things. Not on the warm body nestled against her side. After they'd gotten rid of their plates, it seemed the couch had grown smaller. Or it had developed a hollow in the middle that rolled her toward Gage.

Somehow they'd ended up with their thighs touching.

She wasn't even sure what movie they were watching. People raced after each other, guns went off. A wall exploded, but she'd lost track of the actual plotline as Gage stretched an arm along the back of the couch.

A snicker escaped before she could help it.

He leaned forward slightly. "What?"

"Aren't you supposed to yawn or something before you do that?"

Confusion stretched across his face. She shifted her shoulders, rubbing his biceps softly.

"Ahh." The light went on in his eyes. Gage waggled his brows. "Only if we were teenagers. Now? We're grown-ups. I get to move a little faster."

Oh lordy. Katy's breathing kicked into higher gear.

Gage adjusted position until he held her chin in his fingers.

"Hmmm." His thumb caressed her lower lip. "You said we haven't even had a first kiss."

Katy made an attempt to speak, but no sound emerged. Instead, she licked her lips and tried not to hold her breath. Passing out would be a bad idea right now because she really, really wanted to kiss him.

Gage's gaze danced over her face. "I suppose this is as good a time as any..."

Katy couldn't agree more. She sat motionless as Gage leaned toward her, slowly bringing their lips into contact. A gentle caress of his lips over hers with increasing warmth, increasing pressure. She found her fingers threading their way through his hair, and she was no longer reclining against the back of the couch. No, she was forward on the couch, trying to get as close as possible.

The kiss continued as Gage teased his tongue along her lips, briefly dipping into her mouth before taking everything up a notch.

Katy was no longer warm, she was on fire. His lips left her mouth to dust a series of kisses along her jaw. Teeth nibbled at her earlobe, his tongue delicately tracing the curves of her ear. A shiver shook her from top to bottom as she luxuriated in his careful attention.

Slowly she became aware how tight a clutch she had on his shoulders, desperately tugging him back in an attempt to reconnect their lips.

She found herself being lifted then lowered into his lap, their torsos touching while pleasure wrapped around them like a cozy blanket. She was enjoying herself far too much to protest. Especially when she slid her hands up his chest, palms directly over his rapidly beating heart.

She wanted more. Wanted to straddle him and be able to feel the hardness now nestled against her butt cheek. She wished that solid bit would make contact with other parts of her anatomy. Parts that would very much appreciate more pressure.

With one hand he still controlled her head, lining them up so their lips could mesh perfectly. "Katy," he breathed past her cheek as they separated barely an inch. "Mmm. You taste as good as I remember."

Katy worked to settle her breathing. "I kind of liked it myself."

Then she laughed as Gage pulled his phone from his pocket and clicked on his camera. He grinned at her briefly.

"Gage Jenick, what're you doing?"

"I'm making memories," Gage said. "And I want proof."

He lifted his hand in the air and twisted the camera toward them. A click sounded, and her amusement grew. Selfies. Too funny.

He pulled the phone close and showed her the picture. Her cheeks were flushed, and his eyes glowed with heat. They looked as if they'd been interrupted in the middle of a heavy make-out session, which...*hello*.

Katy was still sitting in his lap. "I can have my second kiss now?"

He tucked away his phone then rested his hand carefully on her thigh, rubbing his thumb back and forth. "I might even be able to work on the third and fourth."

GAGE FOUGHT FOR CONTROL. The urge to sweep Katy up and carry her to the bedroom was strong. They had done that the last time with rather spectacular results, but also incredible consequences. This was not the time for a reen-actment of that evening, no matter how much his body wished for one.

Instead, Gage took it slowly. Appreciated the opportu-nity to reconnect with Katy and hopefully in the process produce some memories. If not of what they had done before, memories for the future.

With her in his lap all warm and soft and willing, it was hard to believe how much different this was than what would have been. What they had enjoyed in September had been fire and lust and youthful innocence in a way. Yes, they'd had sex, and yes, he'd been thinking about it for an awful long time, but it'd been about them. Katy. Gage. About them getting to know each other, and seeing where that relationship might go.

This time, barely three months later, was an entirely different experience. He kissed her, loving how she leaned forward to meet him. How she responded to his caresses as eagerly as he remembered.

He slipped his hand over her hip, gliding gently up to her waist.

Even though her body hadn't changed much yet, this was where everything was different. This is what set tonight apart from what had happened before.

This was no longer a simple relationship between the two of them. There was the baby. Even if he didn't know for sure the baby was his—and *God*, how that tore his soul—the truth still stood. Katy was having a baby. If he went into a relationship with her, he got instant family.

But right now his thoughts were far more on Katy the lover, than Katy the mother-to-be. How far was too far?

His body screamed for him to let a lot more happen. To explore the soft curves under his hands. To use his tongue and lips to see if his memories matched up with the reality he now held.

His mind told him to take it slower.

The sounds she made were not helping. Little gasps of pleasure. Long, low moans that traveled down his spine and reverberated in his balls.

Katy lifted herself, swinging her leg across him to resettle in his lap. She was basically straddling him, and his imagination went wild on all the things the position would allow them to do.

Bright eyes gazed into his as she rested her forearms on his shoulders. She smiled, a dimple appearing in one cheek. "Maybe we should find a better show to watch. This one doesn't seem to be keeping our attention."

He laughed. "I'm trying really hard not to get carried away," he admitted.

"I know." Katy leaned in and grabbed on tight, giving him a huge bear hug. "And I really appreciate it."

They sat like that for a moment, Gage drawing his fingers over her back as he planned the next best move.

A knock on the door jerked their attention upward. She crawled off his lap, and he reluctantly rose to his feet.

"You want to grab us new drinks?" she asked. "I'll get this, then we can watch something else if you want."

Gage had just stepped through the doorway into the kitchen when he heard Katy's quick indrawn breath. He swung around in time to see exactly who was on the other side of the door. All thought of refreshment vanished as he stomped his way back to her side.

"What the hell are you doing here?" he demanded.

Simon's smile vanished as he took in Gage. "I could ask you the same thing."

Katy thrust a hand between the two of them, literally cutting them off from each other.

"Guys, put your dicks back in your pants." She faced Simon, her upper body stiff. "So. Haven't seen you for a couple of weeks. That was quite the appointment you had to run off to."

The dark-haired man on the porch had the grace to look sheepish. "Yeah, sorry about that. Can I come in? I wanted to talk to you..." his gaze shot up to take in Gage as he added, "...privately."

Hell, no. "In your dreams, dickwad."

At his side, Katy sighed heavily. "It would be really nice if I got to be in charge of what happens, since this is my house and all."

She gave Gage a disappointed look, and he backed off only far enough to allow Simon to step into the entranceway.

Simon ignored Gage completely. Instead he took a package from behind his back and offered it to Katy. "I know I was out of line. I shouldn't have taken off on you, or I should have at least phoned. But I've been giving it a lot of thought, and I wanted you to know that I'm there for you. One hundred percent."

The sincerity in Simon's voice seemed real. In fact, Gage had never heard the other man speak so kindly before.

And the Oscar goes to...

Katy twisted the package in her hands. "What is it?"

"Open it and see," Simon teased.

She paced back into the living room, her fingers busily ripping the paper away. Simon's gaze met Gage's, his lips curling in a soundless snarl. That was it—the rivalry was clear. The battle had barely even begun.

"Oh, Simon." She held a fancy baby book in her lap. "It's beautiful."

Simon slipped off his boots and padded across the floor to kneel at her side. "All us kids have one like it that my mom did up for us. I thought you might like to have it while you're pregnant." He turned a few pages in the book. "There are places for you to write things starting now if you want. I hope you like it."

Well, hell. Gage had to admit the other man had more than stepped up to the plate this time. He still didn't trust Simon any farther than he could throw him, but this attentive, caring pretense changed everything.

She ran her fingers over the scrolled gold lettering embossed on the front cover. "Thank you. It's a very considerate gift."

Simon rocked back on his heels. "Maybe you and I could talk about some other things as well."

The tension in her body was clear as she gazed between Gage and Simon. "We do need to talk."

Gage did not want to leave the room. He wasn't going to suggest he should leave the room. In fact, he kind of felt like the only way he would leave the room was if he were dragged from it.

Then, hallelujah, rescue came from the least likely place. Simon's phone went off. He cursed softly as he checked the display before announcing, "Sorry. I have to take this."

"Not to worry," she assured him.

Simon stepped toward the front door to answer his call. Gage took advantage of the moment to sit back beside Katy and place his hand gently on her knee. Reconnecting them.

He ignored the droll voice in his head pointing out he was staking his claim. "How are you doing?"

She made a face. "This is not what I expected to happen tonight. Not at all."

Gage watched Simon as he spoke on his phone. Dammit, he didn't want to do this, but he had to offer. "What do you want me to do?"

Katy sighed. She leaned back on the couch and stared at the ceiling. "I don't know what I want anymore."

Her comment jerked a brief snort of amusement from him. "Right, that was a load of bullshit."

A snicker escaped her. "Yeah, well, how about I don't know what I want at this moment."

He spoke softly. "How about I admit I don't want to leave you here with him."

She glanced over the couch then back at Gage. "I can't kick him out. He has just as much right to be involved as you do."

There was something wrong with her reasoning, but Gage hadn't yet figured out the best way to tell her that without sounding like an A-one asshole or a jealous fool. Both of which titles he probably could claim. "You don't have to do anything tonight."

She nodded, the heated passion they had shared from earlier rising briefly to her eyes as she stared at him.

"Katy, can I get together with you later?" Simon interrupted the moment. "One of my crew was looking over the material list we have to send to the supplier, and he thinks there are problems. I have to check tonight if we need to make changes, because they're filling the order tomorrow."

"You want to meet for coffee at the café tomorrow?" she asked.

Gage wondered if he should stake out one of the neighboring booths.

Simon paused. "I can get away for lunch on Monday. If you can be there at noon?"

When she nodded, Simon slipped his boots back on and placed a hand on the doorknob.

Instant decision time.

"I have to go as well," Gage announced. He stood and paced past Katy, ignoring the shock on her face.

But hanging around any longer wasn't going to help, not with the walls she'd slapped up as soon as Simon had appeared bearing gifts. Besides, there was something he had to do.

"Thanks for all your help today." Katy handed him his toolbox.

"Thanks for dinner."

They stood awkwardly as Simon looked on. Then Gage figured what the hell, leaned in and kissed her. Right smack-dab on the lips. He pulled back before he could get lost in the act, though, tipping a finger to his forehead and giving her a wink.

He turned toward a very stern-faced Simon who left the house ahead of him at a near run. Asshole probably had an idea what was coming.

Gage had to move quickly to catch up to the man before he got his truck door shut and locked. Gage wrapped his fingers around the doorframe and jerked it all the way open.

"Seems strange you're that gung-ho all of a sudden about Katy and the baby."

Simon sneered, all the pleasantness he'd shown earlier vanishing like snow hitting a hot stovepipe. "I don't give a shit what you think, Jenick, so fuck off."

He attempted to pull his door shut, but Gage had his arm firmly in place, and nobody was going nowhere until he was done his say. "I promised Katy I wouldn't go around her decisions, but I'm warning you. Do anything to hurt her, physically or otherwise, and I will take you apart one piece at a time."

He slammed the door shut with enough force to make Simon's eardrums ring. Gage didn't care. He was already halfway across the yard to his own vehicle, fighting to keep the fire inside from flaring even higher.

Handing out a caution was one thing, but actually taking his tire iron to the other man's vehicle would be pushing it a little far. Especially when he noticed Katy standing in the window watching them both.

The possessive feelings growing inside could tear him apart if he wasn't careful, but he wasn't sure he could turn them off anymore.

CHAPTER 11

Simon met her at the café, all sincere and contrite for having taken off for weeks without a word.

He'd brought her flowers. Roses. Like a dozen long-stemmed red roses that made her feel uncomfortable, especially when she realized everyone around them had gotten an eyeful and were whispering furiously. This gift wasn't like the baby book; it was as if he was stamping his mark on her.

And hothouse roses? Not really her thing.

"I needed to get my head straightened out," he explained. "It was a shock, but I'm ready to face my responsibilities."

He reached for her hand. Katy grabbed her water glass and curled her fingers around it to remain safely on her side of the table. Might as well get the worst part of the conversation over with early. "I've decided to wait with the paternal testing until after the baby is born."

Disapproval streaked his face so briefly before a smile replaced it she was left wondering if she was imagining things.

Simon shrugged. "If that's what you want, I'm okay with it."

He leaned back in his chair and looked her over, and it wasn't like when Gage did it. No rush of pleasure streamed to any of her body parts. Instead, Katy held herself in control.

"You want to go to a movie tonight?" he asked.

Drat. After his high-class desertion he still expected her to date him? "I'm...seeing Gage."

This time there was no mistaking his frown. "But I told you we'd gotten back together."

"It's been a while since then, and life has changed. Gage and I are dating now."

"But you might be pregnant with my baby." He shook his head. "You should be with me, not him."

If she had to repeat this many more times, she was going to start bouncing off the walls. "Enough. This is not up for debate, Simon. What we need to talk about is if you want to be around, if you are the dad—"

"Then I want to be around," he snapped. "Of course."

Dammit. Could nothing go easy? Katy nodded slowly. "If you want to wait until we know for sure..."

He gave her an intent smile. "Hell no. I want to be with you now, Katy. So that means anything you need."

Right. She tossed out the ultimate test. "Then I'll let you know when my prenatal classes are, and stuff like that."

"I'll be there." He lowered his voice. "I'm always available to you, sugar. Anytime you need me, you give me a call. And you be careful with Gage."

Careful? "What's that supposed to mean?"

Simon leaned across the table. "There are things about that man that don't line up. I'm worried about you being with him."

Katy laughed. "I think it's okay. He's been around for a long time. We pretty much know everything there is to know."

The waitress showed up and took their order, and in some ways the rest of the meal passed okay. Simon was attentive, and polite, and a touch...unreal. As if he was playing a part.

Or maybe it was her discomfort in finding herself in another out-of-control situation. Two guys paying attention to her. The baby. Dealing with her continued mental changes.

Somewhere along the line she had to get a break.

Katy paid for half the lunch bill, fighting to keep it on a "not date" footing. Simon took off back to the construction site he was working. "I'll call you later to figure out when we can get together."

Oh joy.

"Hey, Katy."

Across the café a group waved her down. She said goodbye to Simon and gratefully escaped.

"Your brother done working on my car yet?" Older fellow. The face was familiar, but the man's name escaped Katy.

Another annoying byproduct of her accident—names were like ghostly creatures, flitting in and out of her memory at the least convenient times. And she was sick of asking names only to get a huge disappointed frown and be informed she was talking to someone she'd known her entire life.

Screw repeating that embarrassment. Instead, Katy smiled big and faked it. Surely she'd get a clue from his response. "You know what? I'm headed back to the shop right now. I'll check how it's going, then give you a call."

The guy nodded. "My new cell number is on the work order, and you know my home number."

Drat. Foiled again. She walked into the cold winter air and wrapped her coat a little closer around her. The December sky was clear, and her breath escaped in small puffs of white. It was far too pretty out to stay frustrated, even with Simon and her brain being annoying.

She could deal with this. She'd just describe the guy to Clay, and he'd know who it was.

The bell over the shop door rang as she stepped into the warmth of the Thompson and Sons customer area. The front desk was empty, so she stuck her head through the door to the workshop hangar to shout a warning before anyone rushed to answer the summons.

"Just me. I'm back from lunch."

Why did her gaze have to automatically find Gage where he squatted near the front of a vehicle working on a bumper?

Why did he have to be staring back with that intense expression that made her knees shaky?

She escaped to discard her coat on a side table in the office. Slowly she'd figured out how to do the paperwork and expense tracking, but it was still a struggle making the numbers line up. It was her job, though, so she'd find a way, even if numbers made her jittery.

A couple phone calls later, she remembered the mystery man in the café and returned to the workshop.

"Clay? There's a guy I met at lunch who wanted to know when his job would be done. Older man, receding grey hair and fairly thin face."

Her brother wiped his hands on a cloth, his lopsided grin taunting her. "That describes about eighty percent of the owners we're working on stuff for. You got anything more for me to go on, like, oh...a name?"

She shook her head. "Sorry."

Then Gage was there, all large and looming and far too sexy in his coverall. How a bit of grease and dust could increase his appeal was unfair. "Memory lapse?"

"Let's pretend I got memory wiped by aliens. That would make it simpler."

Gage laughed, his arm curling around her waist to hug her gently. "We need code words and secret signals to use in these cases."

His lighthearted response soothed her edgy nerves, and it wasn't so upsetting anymore. "Hang on—I've got an idea."

She dropped the notepad in her hand on the hood of the nearest car and went to work. Maybe a pen wasn't the best tool, but it still worked. The man's face appeared before her in inky blue on the lined paper.

Only a few moments later when she held out the sketch to Clay, the shop had gone silent. None of her brothers were working—they had all gathered around her.

Katy glanced at them, puzzled. "What?"

Clay cleared his throat. "When did you learn how to do that?"

"Do what?"

Gage took the notepad from her, staring at the page with a huge grin on his face. "Draw pictures so lifelike I'd swear that Steve Berkhold is about to wink at us. Katy, this is amazing."

She shrugged. "That's who needs to be called about the job."

"But you can't draw," Troy informed her. "You nearly flunked art in junior high."

"Bullshit. How can you flunk art?" Gage asked.

Troy had taken the notepad from her and held it up to admire the sketch. "Ask her, but somehow she managed. I remember the conversations at the dinner table."

"You remember them because you were thankful someone other than you was getting in shit about their report card." Mitch tousled Katy's hair then paced backward to return to his task. "That was the year Troy spent more time skipping English class than attending, right?"

"Fuck off. Not only was that a long time ago, but you were out rebuilding bike engines when you should have been in class as well." Troy handed the book back to Katy. "Nice picture. And you did have a lower grade than me."

"Ass." Katy rested her fists on her hips. "Go away. We're not teenagers anymore."

Clay went to call Steve, leaving Katy alone with Gage. He leaned back on the railing, arms crossed easily in front of him as he smiled at her.

There was a streak of dirt on his cheek, and without thinking she wiped it away with her thumb.

He snuck an arm around her and lightly tugged her against his body. "So, you're a budding da Vinci, are you?"

She peeked over her shoulder, but shockingly, no one was watching them. "You're being awful forward. You don't think manhandling me in the garage is a bad idea with all my brothers around?"

"First, I'm not manhandling you, I'm hugging you. And second, your brothers need to get used to the idea that we're a couple. They're big boys. They can handle it."

She laid the notebook on his chest and crossed her hands over it, enjoying the close position far more than she wanted to admit. "So we're a couple now?"

His hand made slow circles on her back. "We don't

need to repeat this conversation. Yes, we're a couple. Deal with it."

A laugh bubbled up. In spite of her frustrations, there were a few silver linings beginning to appear. "Hey, Gage. Did you know I could draw?"

"Hmm, you going to draw me sometime?"

Oh, lordy, the images that flooded her brain were far too triple X. Naked Gage. All the long, hard muscles she was currently leaning against glistening with water fresh out of a shower. Or better yet, slick from a hard workout, muscles pumped up and heated.

"You look as if you like that idea." Gage leaned closer and whispered by her ear, "You want it, you got it. Need to explore this new talent of yours, and I'm game to be of service any way I can."

Not only did it appear she had miraculously learned how to draw overnight, but his words threw her into a sexual heat wave—the images far too vivid.

"You want to service me?" she teased, shocked by her boldness.

"Oh hell, yeah." He nuzzled the side of her neck lightly before drawing a deep breath and reluctantly separating them. "Only later. Back to work for us both."

She stepped away from him, sad at the loss of warmth, but highly pleased by the fact that when she turned in the doorway of the office he was still watching her.

CHAPTER 12

Janey insisted she should be Katy's primary support during labour, and Gage agreed it made the most sense.

"She's your best friend, and you know you're going to want her around, no matter what." Gage got a look of approval from Janey for that one.

The fact his suggestion pissed Simon off pleased him even more. It felt good to jerk the other man's chain.

"I don't need three coaches," Katy complained. "If Janey comes with me to classes, I'll be fine."

"But I want to be there," Gage insisted.

As soon as Simon heard Gage was going, he wanted to come as well. So they were *all* at the hospital, like one big happy family. Regular classes wouldn't start until later in the new year, but for some reason the first get-together was now, nearly six months before Katy's expected D-Day.

Which meant Gage had to play nice. He did his best to ignore Simon, but the other man was right there in his face all the time. Deliberate, too. Gage saw it. The subtle glances as Simon assessed when would be the best moment to step in and cut off Gage and Janey.

If it wasn't for Katy in the middle, Gage would have been tempted to simply drag Simon outside and duct tape him to a fence somewhere.

"Tonight is a chance for you to meet a few other couples who are expecting their first babies. Along with providing you with nutritional and exercise information, we'll exchange a phone list so you first-time moms can get some support from others who are in the same situation." The nurse teaching the session glanced around the room, her smile stuttering when it passed over their mob of four occupying the corner they'd staked out. "Umm. Right. So we're not worrying about breathing exercises yet, but we have booked a tour of the hospital."

Gage followed along as the nurse led them through sign-in procedure, and what documents were needed. She showed them the elevators and the stairs to the obstetrics floor. "In case one of you is running late," the nurse teased. "With cell phones we find less partners are missing delivery than in the old days, but waiting for the elevator can seem to take forever if you are in a rush."

Someone asked about emergency procedures, and the tension in the entire group rose.

Gage held on tight to Katy's elbow. He'd wiggled his way past Simon on the last room change—okay, he'd basically shoved himself past the guy to steal the spot at her side. He ignored Simon's growl of frustration, instead concentrating on Katy.

He leaned in close enough to whisper in her ear. "You're going to do fine, having the baby."

She squeezed his arm. "Easy for you to say. You don't have to push a football out through your private parts."

The urge to cover his groin hit hard and fast. "No, thank God."

A loud snort of amusement escaped her, and she hid her face against him as the entire class swung to look at them, distracted from the serious discussion about C-sections and epidurals.

Their guide opened a door and gestured the class into a new space. "And these are the birthing rooms. Chances are you'll spend more time walking the hallways or at home than here, but we're pleased to have renovated these recently. You can see you have a private space with a shower and an easy chair for whoever is supporting you to rest, if needed." Another glance back at the convoy from the nurse, as if she was wondering how they were going to deal with all those bodies in the room.

Gage had his fingers crossed that by the time June arrived, Simon would be out of the picture.

"The bed adjusts in height and angle, so once you're ready to push, we simply slip these stirrups into position..." she demonstrated, picking up a set of poster boards from the bed as she turned back to the class, "...and we're all ready to go. Here's what point you'll be at when you are ready for actual delivery."

Maybe he was a prude, but the picture the nurse held was not something he wanted to look at in public. Definitely not in a mixed group. Gage had watched porn, and seen his share of pussies up close and personal, but staring at some woman he didn't know with a baby right *there*?

"Oh, God, someone *help*."

Gage glanced to the right to discover Simon's face had gone totally white, the man wavering on his feet as Janey attempted to keep him vertical. Tempting as it was to ignore the call for assistance, Gage stepped forward and caught Simon before the man folded to the ground in a dead faint.

"Relax, everyone." The nurse put down the picture and gestured everyone out of the room. "Let's give him some air. Head to the right and we'll visit the nursery."

She paused beside Simon who sat on the floor with his head between his knees. "Are you okay here for a bit?"

Gage couldn't resist, even though this might get him killed. "Janey can stay with him until he recovers," he suggested.

Janey made a hideous face at him behind the nurse's back. "Sure, why don't you all go ahead, and we'll catch up."

He owed her big-time, but totally took advantage as he guided Katy down the hall. They stopped in front of the glass windows looking in on the few babies sleeping in the maternity ward. The nurse did her little spiel about the area, and the class moved on, but Katy remained motionless, just staring.

"You okay?" Gage cradled her close, more interested in her reactions than looking at some strangers' babies.

She didn't say anything for a moment, then nodded. "Yeah."

Only she was quiet the entire trip back to her house. He stoked the fire while she changed into a pair of soft sweat-pants with a loose T-shirt. He sat on the couch, and when Katy crawled next to him and cuddled up, something inside dared to come alive.

She leaned against his chest as she stared into the fire. "I really miss my mom."

Gage worked to keep his breathing even, relishing the contact between them. "Meg was a terrific lady, and a great mom. You're going to be just like her. You *are* like her."

Katy tilted her head back, dark brown eyes capturing

him and not letting him go. "I hope so. Even a little, because she left a mark on me. I wish she was here for this." She laid her hand on her belly. She had a tiny little swell, barely there.

Gage couldn't stop himself. His hand joined hers, linking their fingers and putting the warmth of her belly against his knuckles. "She'd be proud of you. I know she would be."

"Even though I'm knocked up?" Only she smiled, softening the words. "Yeah, I think Mom would be okay with it, though it's a little unorthodox. She loved all kids."

"I know. I got to have some of that love directed my way as well." Gage paused. "She filled a hole in my heart I'd had ever since my own mom died."

Katy stilled, gaze darting over his face. "You never talked about your folks."

Gage shook his head. "It wasn't something I wanted to discuss. And even as a kid I knew what the rumour mill would do with the story."

A line folded between her brows. "Something bad happen, Gage?"

He kissed her temple. "It's not something to talk about at the end of a long day."

She shook her head. "Important things need to be shared, though."

It was damn near impossible to get the words out, no matter how right she was. This was important, and he had to tell her, and soon, but his old fears came to the surface. What if he shared and that made the entire house of cards fall down around him?

Only telling her had to happen, and now would be better than later. The quiet intimacy of the moment, plus her honesty regarding her mother loosened his lips. "It's a bit of a nightmare. My dad was a long-haul trucker while Mom stayed home with me. He'd been out on a hunting trip with some friends and came home to discover her in the process of packing. Straight-out announced she wanted a divorce. She'd found someone else."

Katy's eyes widened. "Oh. Not good."

"Not good at all." How much should he share? "My father didn't believe her at first, but she insisted. Guess she'd found out he wasn't being faithful either, but the two of them screaming at each other on the front lawn was the first time I knew anything."

"How old were you?"

Gage took a deep breath. "Twelve. Old enough to understand what they were screaming about. Old enough that I knew it was getting ugly."

She squeezed his fingers, but didn't say anything.

One slow exhale let him continue. "He didn't want her to go. I don't know if it was because he was jealous or what, but he kept begging her not to leave. She just kept shoving bags into the car."

Katy wasn't breathing.

Gage stared at the fire. "It might have turned out okay. I mean, horrid and terrible and everything else, but she told me to get in the car, and that's when he lost it. Said she wasn't taking his son from him as well."

"Oh no."

Gage pulled in his courage and looked Katy in the eye. "My mom told him I wasn't his son. She'd gotten pregnant when he was on a run one time, and my early arrival was an excuse. I was another man's son, and she was damn well taking me with her."

Silence. Katy's lips were pinched together tightly, her usually glowing skin gone white.

Yeah. Pretty much explained a lot of things.

Gage had to look away from her clear gaze. Had to finish—not all of it, but at least the next part of the story. "He went a little crazy. Started hitting her, and by the time he was stopped, she'd been hurt so bad she died a couple days later."

Katy curled her fingers around his back as she leaned in and hugged him, as if attempting to comfort the child he'd been. "And you ended up in foster care."

She was shaking, and he couldn't bear to tell her the rest. Instead he buried his guilt and stroked her hair, the softness soothing him deep inside. "Yeah. It wasn't that bad. There are a lot of good people who take in kids. Only by that age I wasn't as cute, and there are less people who want teens, so I got moved around a bit."

Less people who wanted to deal with the aftermath of a twelve-year-old who had been through what he'd seen.

What he'd done.

Katy pulled back, her eyes bright with unshed tears. "I'm so sorry that happened, but I'm glad you ended up in Rocky."

Her warm palm cupped his face, and she leaned in slowly to kiss him. Not a sympathy move, but highlighting the growing connection between them. Giving a touch of herself in offering, expecting something from him in return.

What he gave her was control. Instead of turning the softness into a ravishing, he kept his hands from roaming and concentrated on kissing her. At least he did until she caught his fingers and tugged. Pressed his palm against her breast and held it there.

She had nothing on under the T-shirt, and her nipple tightened, poking his palm as their lips continued to meet. He went with it, stroking gently, cupping the full round and teasing her nipple with his thumb until she arched toward him.

God, the noises she made as he kissed his way down her neck. He twisted her against the couch and jerked up her shirt, exposing her breasts.

Exploring all her soft skin was not a hardship. The only thing hard was his cock, imprisoned behind his jeans where he fully intended on keeping it for another night.

This was about touching Katy. Seeing the changes in her body since the last time they'd been together. Delighting in the opportunity to be with her physically.

Making memories.

He kissed the top of her soft curves held in his hand, pausing to glance into her eyes. Katy's mouth hung slightly open as her breathing quickened.

"You're so beautiful."

She smiled, and he dipped his head to kiss her lips quickly before returning to torment her nipple. A lick around the tip, a gentle blow of air until it tightened. Pregnancy gave her skin a flush and increased the size of her breasts.

"Oh. *Oh*, careful."

He gently rolled the tip with his tongue. "More sensitive."

"You're making me wet without even touching my pussy," Katy confessed.

"I'll pet your pussy later." As long as she was squirming with pleasure he was doing something right.

Unexpectedly, Katy took control. She wiggled out of her sweatpants and lay back on the couch, pulling him over her. Only this time she directed his hand over her belly and between her legs.

Gage smiled against her lips as he stroked the narrow line of elastic. "You're a lot bolder these days. I like it."

"Shut up and kiss me," Katy demanded, but she was smiling as well.

The kissing was easy. Nothing soft anymore, he consumed her hungrily. Stroked and tasted and took in every one of her gasps and moans like a symphony of lust.

At the same time he slipped his fingers under the edge of her panties, forcing the fabric to one side so he could ease between her folds into slick wetness.

"Oh, yes." Katy pressed up into his hand.

"Eager." He wasn't going to wait. But slow was good for another reason—this time to bring her to the point of maximum pleasure. One finger parted her carefully, easing inside her tight passage. His thumb centered over her clit with gentle pressure as Katy clutched his head and pulled him back far enough she could stare into his eyes.

A second finger joined the first. Her face registered the additional pressure, and she widened her legs. Her tongue slipped out to wet her lips, and her breathing sped up as he moved a little quicker, fingertips curled slightly to find the spot he wanted. Again and again he thrust into her, checking her response, loving how she accepted the pleasure and soaked it in. Embraced it, and with one swoop, exploded in climax, her body squeezing his fingers tightly as her eyes closed.

"*Gage.*"

"Hmm, nice." He slowed his touch. Took her down easily as her body continued to shake from her orgasm. "God, you're beautiful when you come."

She melted onto the couch, boneless relaxation over-taking her. "No pictures, okay? I think I can remember this happened, in all its Technicolor glory."

Gage laughed then kissed her. Eased back as she sat up.

"What now?" Katy asked, all flushed and warm.

"Now you get dressed, and I'll tuck you into bed."

It obviously wasn't what she expected to hear. Katy damn near pouted. "Alone?"

He nodded. "This time."

"When is next time? Soon?"

His body ached. "Very soon, but this is about more than sex, Katy. We're memory making. Finding out more about each other. Let's not rush too fast."

"Uh-uh. You said soon. So, while yes to those other things, I think soon should mean soon. Promise?" Katy pulled her clothing back into line as ordered, but she still looked wonderfully near ravished as she stumbled to her feet.

He shot upward to steady her. Anticipation of growing closer in so many ways thrilled him more than he could say.

"I promise." When she was ready, he would be as well. Oh, hell yeah.

CHAPTER 13

She'd figured it out. Gage was determined to drive her crazy. Either that or he'd been taken over by aliens, and the body snatchers had forgotten to program the clone for sex.

No, that wasn't right. Katy was still getting orgasms, lots of them, delivered in a timely and most enthusiastic fashion on a regular basis. The man's tongue should be enshrined—when it came to going down on her, he was talented and thorough enough she couldn't walk afterward.

Actual sex was the issue. Sex hadn't yet happened, and after three weeks of exploring lots of other pleasurable activities, Katy was more than eager.

She was pissed.

On the nonsexual side, her unsatisfied libido had her directing frustrated energy into a variety of art projects. She couldn't seem to stop herself. The fight with numbers had turned into an addiction with creativity. As the baby growing inside started to make itself more apparent, her interest in things she had never tried before continued. Her brothers had been thrilled at the suggestion of getting her gift cards from craft shops for Christmas. After a few enthusiastic shopping sprees, she had knitting projects started, and a quilt. She'd bought coloured pencils and art pads for her doodles.

The last trip to the store had ended with her buying an assortment of Play-Doh and clay that she was itching to dive into. Around the house new hobbies lay scattered on all available surfaces.

The phone rang, pulling her from her current art project. She checked the call display and sighed her frustration before answering.

"Simon. What's up?" And it had better not be another invitation for a date.

He chuckled. This annoying, grating sound. "Got a present for you, sugar. Just making sure you're home so I can bring it over."

Katy leaned on the wall by the kitchen and fought to keep her voice level. "I don't need any more presents, Simon. Please, stop trying to buy your way into my affections."

He'd bailed out of the prenatal experience after that disastrous first day, but for the rest, he just wouldn't give up. He called. He dropped in. She was polite each time she turned him down, but he kept on coming like some crazy Red Bull-fueled boyfriend from hell.

"You don't mean that, I know you don't."

"Oh, yes, I'm sure I do. Gage and I are happy"—happy enough except for the fact she was going to kill him if he didn't get a move on—"and I need you to wait until we know more in terms of the baby."

"I think you need a little more convincing, is all," Simon insisted. "We were good together, and we need to be together."

"You should stop calling me." The doorbell rang, and Katy turned to answer it. "We are not getting together."

The man didn't give up. "Who's at the door? Is it Gage? You shouldn't be with him. I swear he's dangerous."

Katy peeked outside to discover Gage waiting for her. "He's not dangerous, and you're getting annoying. I have to go. I'll be in touch if I need anything."

"I'll—"

She hung up on Simon and pulled the door open for Gage. How the man managed to make a winter coat and toque look sexy was damn unfair. "Hi."

He straightened from his easy slouch. "Hi. Can I come in?"

Katy shrugged. "Suit yourself."

She turned back to her project, pretending to ignore him, but she knew he was there, all right. Just was tired of his bossy ass, along with the continued annoyance of Simon.

Silence loomed until she finally peeked over her shoulder.

"Why are you still wearing all your snow gear?"

Gage shrugged. "It's a nice day. I wanted to go for a walk."

For some reason his wording only upset her more. "Fine. Have a nice time."

She turned her back and ripped a page violently from the magazine, examining it for the best section to add to her mosaic.

Cold fabric wrapped around her as he leaned against her back. "You mad at me?"

"I thought you were walking."

"With you, Katy. I want to go for a walk with you."

"That's not what you said," Katy pointed out snarkily. "And far be it for me to insert myself into your plans."

125

VIVIAN AREND

Gage lifted her from the chair and forced her chin up. "Okay, point taken. Will you come with me? It's pretty outside, and we should take advantage of the nice weather."

Like some damn yo-yo, her mood rose instantly. Katy couldn't hold on to her mad. "I'd love to go for a walk. Give me a minute to change."

Thirty minutes later they were strolling through the birch trees at the edge of the town park, the snowy path underfoot packed down by a snowmobile. The crisp January air burned her throat slightly as she breathed, but it was still refreshing. Snow clung to bare branches, shimmering white against the shockingly blue Alberta sky.

Gage had her hand in his, their gloves separating them but connected just the same. "You look like you're having a ton of fun with the crafts. And sewing. And painting."

"Post-concussion syndrome. Doctor finally gave me a name."

"Really? That's cool."

"Yeah. I suppose. The brain's a neat thing. I damaged part of it, so now the pathways or whatever shifted in new directions and *poof*, I'm an *arteest*."

"Creativity everywhere."

His comment hit the wrong way.

"I know my house is a mess," Katy snapped, then instantly felt guilty.

He squeezed her fingers. "I didn't say anything about the house. Don't jump to conclusions."

"But it is a mess, and that's not like me, but dammit..." Katy jerked her hand free and paced to the edge of the trail, staring at the sky as she attempted to find her sense of peace. "My God, this is insane."

He had the guts to laugh softly. "Katy, I'm not judging you. Or expecting anything from you—"

126

"Yeah? Well maybe you should."

That dangerous grin of his widened. "Oh?"

Ass. "Is there something wrong with my body, Gage? You afraid of hurting the baby if we have sex? I mean, you can't be afraid that I'll get pregnant, because, hello, that ship has already sailed."

Jumping from arts and crafts to sex in under a minute. *Go, Katy!*

"You're not happy with our sex life?" Gage asked.

A growl escaped her. She marched across the short distance between them to get in his face. "We don't have a sex life. We have you deciding when to turn off the heat, and I'm getting tired of it."

"Agreed."

His instant response pierced her bubble and deflated part of her anger. "You agree? Then why are you being such a pain in the butt?"

Gage pulled off his glove and cupped his warm palm to her cheek. "You know how you wanted to be invited along on the walk? Not just me assuming that you would come?"

"Yeah?" Where was this going?

He stroked a thumb over her cheek. "You have changed since the accident, and I like the new Katy. I like how she's bolder, and more outspoken. I think it's fascinating that you've suddenly got this artistic side, but there's one thing you're not doing."

She nuzzled against his hand, placated a little. "And what's that, bossypants?"

A low rumble of amusement escaped him. "You're still not deciding what you want then going for it."

There was a twist she hadn't expected. "I thought you said I was bolder?"

"You are...and you aren't." Gage enclosed her in his

VIVIAN AREND

arms. "You're bold as brass for a moment then you cut back like your response is a bad thing. It's not, Katy. If you want something, take it. If you don't want something, stop beating around the bush. Tell him to get lost."

Oh. "This is about Simon."

Gage shrugged. "Partly. I know you're worried about him being the dad, but since you're not planning on marrying the guy, maybe you should stop being so accommodating."

She'd thought of that, but... "You're right, but it's still a tough step to take."

"Not saying it would be easy, but what's the use of having this new attitude if you're not going to use it?"

Katy slipped her hands around his neck. "Well, if you insist, I can think of something I'd really like to do."

"Hmm." Gage stroked her cheek. "Go on, Katybug, boss me around and get some practice."

They couldn't get back to the house fast enough.

But when they arrived, Katy didn't simply demand he take her into the bedroom. No matter how daring she felt that was one step further than she could take right now.

There was something else she could do...

"Take off your clothes," she ordered.

He lifted one brow, but his hands went to his buttons. "I like how this is starting."

She grabbed her drawing pad and a set of charcoal pencils, and his expression fell.

A laugh escaped her. "You should see your face right now."

His shirt was open, sliding from his shoulders. "This is your call, Katy. Take what you want."

Oh, she had every intention of it.

She rotated the easy chair, sitting to enjoy the view as

Gage continued to strip. No fancy dance moves, just honest-to-goodness, solidly built and one-hundred-percent-naked male being revealed in her living room.

She stared at the curve of muscles across his shoulders. The flare of his biceps and lovely firm chest. He stood with his arms crossed, seemingly at ease in spite of being naked. Well-defined stomach muscles, that V-line muscle framing his lower abdomen.

His cock nestled in a thatch of dark hair.

Katy's fingers flew over the page, her gaze darting back and forth between the picture and her model. She was going to be drooling in about thirty seconds if she wasn't careful.

It took an amazingly short time to put on the page the sex-on-legs that was Gage.

"Out of curiosity, you putting a fig leaf over my cock?" he asked.

"No." Although, she wasn't sure how to draw that part of his anatomy. It had most definitely changed appearance since he'd stripped, rising to a length she longed to explore more closely. "You're making it tough, dude. When I said nothing moves, you didn't listen very well, did you now?"

A burst of laughter escaped him. "I guess not."

Katy abandoned the drawing materials behind her and rose to her feet. "I need to get hands-on for this next part."

Gage smiled, but said nothing.

It was like being in a candy store for grown-ups. She slid her hands over his arms and across his chest, savouring the warmth. The scratch of hair on his limbs against her palms. The rapid beat of his heart under her fingers as she explored his chest, pressing a kiss to the center of his torso.

"I think you should get naked as well," Gage suggested, his voice low and husky.

She thought about it for a second. "I'd like that."

He was over her in a second, helping her strip. Pulling off clothes and touching her everywhere, and this was what she'd longed for. Both of them involved, kisses pressed over heated skin, hands touching intimately.

She wrapped her fingers around his cock and stroked, loving the softness of his skin in contrast to the hardness beneath. Gage covered her hand with his and increased the pressure, guiding her as his torso tightened, moans of pleasure escaping his lips.

A slow bend brought her close enough to lick the head of his cock, her tongue tracing the slit, teasing him. He let her play, one hand holding his shaft so she could access the head, wetting him briefly before covering him with her mouth and sucking lightly.

"You've got about ten seconds before I blow," Gage warned.

Katy pulled back with a *pop* as she released him. "Hair trigger?"

"It's been a while."

The realization it had been months since he said they'd had sex hit in a rush. "You've been abstaining for too long."

He went willingly with her into the bedroom. One firm push on his chest toppled him to the bed, and she crawled on top.

The pregnancy had begun to affect her body, but she loved the changes so far. Better skin, more sensitive breasts, just the trace of rounding to her belly.

Gage ran his hands over her as she straddled his hips, obviously enjoying the changes as well. "Whatever you want. I'm yours."

Katy rocked herself over his cock, pressing the hard ridge against her clit repetitively. Smooth strokes that slowly brought up her pleasure and seemed to please Gage as well. He held on to her hips and helped her move, his eyes pinned to her chest as her breasts swayed.

Then she couldn't wait any longer. Katy lifted her hips and directed him into her core. Her hand brushed Gage's as he held his cock upright, and their fingers connected as she slowly eased herself down. One rock after another as she opened around him, taking his thick shaft into her body.

"Sweet mercy, Katy. So good."

She paused, filled completely, squeezing lightly to enjoy the sensation. Testing for pain, or anything that worried her, but all that registered was pleasure. Connection.

An itch to be scratched...*now*.

She shifted over him. Rose and fell with increasing tempo until she was at the edge of exploding. Gage cupped her breasts, lightly pinching her nipples, and she gasped at the streak of ecstasy that washed through her system.

Gage caught her by the hips and raised her slightly.

"Stay there," he ordered, waiting for her to get into position. As soon as she obeyed, he thrust upward, increasing the pressure, the speed. One hand slipped down to touch her clit, thumb firmly in position over the sensitive point. He rocked his cock in and out of her body until she shattered.

Waves rolled her from the inside out, heavy and lingering from having been so long in the making. Anticipation had nothing on the reality, as he continued to fuck her through her orgasm, finally clamping down on her hips as she caught her breath. He jerked upright, his cock deep as he came. Another set of aftershocks rocked her core, leaving her head spinning and body swaying with pleasure.

He curled up and caught her against his chest, kissing her face, running his fingers over her back. They sat there for a long time, intimately connected, until their breathing got back to something near normal.

Gage stroked her cheek. "Was that what you were hoping for?"

"Hmm." Katy rested her head on his shoulder, kissing his neck lightly. "I think so. We might have to try it again later, just to make sure."

"If that's what you want."

They laughed together, slowly coming down off the high.

Katy felt different inside. Not the sex, but in taking another step forward. She might have lost some of her memories, but she was making new ones. She might have lost some of herself, but the new her wasn't that bad of a person.

And the guy currently touching her like she was beautiful, precious and amazing? He wasn't hard to accept as a part of the new life she was facing.

132

CHAPTER 14

February

Gage rolled over carefully. The moonlight shining in the window fell across Katy's face, high-lighting her relaxed curves as she slept. He stroked her bangs off her forehead, unable to keep a smile off his face as he touched her.

Making love with the woman rocked him to his soul, but these moments were somehow even more intense. The quiet times when he'd look up to catch her smiling at him. The pauses before she'd shyly agree to let him stay the night.

For the past month he could confidently say they'd been a real couple. No Simon intruding, no lingering worries about what had happened before. Just building something special here and now.

It was happening, ever so slowly. Falling in love—he was sure of it. His fears faded as they spent more time together.

Her eyes opened, giving him another glimpse of shining and happy Katy. "You're staring."

"You're supposed to be asleep," he chastised. "You have a lot to do tomorrow, remember?"

Katy crawled out of bed. "Tell that to the future trampoline star in my belly. I need to pee."

Watching her ass wiggle as she slipped into the bathroom got his motor rolling all over again, but he really shouldn't ravish her three times in one night.

She crawled back into bed and straight into his arms, twisting their limbs together to plant her chilled feet on his calves.

"Hey, that's not nice."

Katy grinned. "You comfy?"

Hell yeah. "Nothing to complain about."

He kissed her nose, then embraced her. Soft heat. Wonderful connection. Gage was falling hard, and he wasn't going to try to stop it anymore.

He was hovering on the edge of sleep when the familiar nighttime noises changed. A vehicle passed by, motor growling, but instead of fading, the sound got louder. Lights flickered on the wall of Katy's bedroom, slowly increasing in strength.

A horn rang, blasting through the night air.

Katy blinked awake as Gage rolled out of bed, cautiously stepping beside the window. "What's happening?" she asked sleepily.

"Not sure." Gage pulled back the curtains. The powerful front lights of a truck blinded him. "Shit."

"Fucking bastard." The cries came from outside, faint, but getting louder. "Asshole. Get away from her."

Katy was on her feet, reaching for her robe. "Is that Simon?"

A loud rattle was followed by shattering glass. The window beside Gage's head exploded into a starry mess of cracks an instant before it imploded, pieces of glass falling to the floor and the edge of the bed. Katy screamed.

From outside Simon shouted, "Get out of her house, you murderer."

Another crash sounded as a second window was destroyed. Gage dodged past the glass to drag Katy into the safety of the hall. "Stay here," he ordered, ducking back into the bedroom to snatch up his jeans.

She had grabbed her robe, wrapping the material around herself as Gage jerked on his pants and headed to the front door to find his shoes. "Wait, what are you doing? Gage."

"Call 911. Simon's gone insane. Damn idiot."

Katy had the phone in her hand. "Calling. Don't go out there."

Another crash echoed as the bathroom window was destroyed. If he didn't go out, Simon was likely to take out every single piece of glass in the house. Gage pointed firmly at Katy. "Stay here, and get the RCMP."

He opened the door cautiously, glancing around the corner to make sure Simon wasn't waiting to jump him.

The man stood a few feet from the house, his truck pushed through the snow bank with its high-beam lights directed into the busted windows. Simon roared obscenities, hurling a beer can that bounced off the wood siding and disappeared into the shadows.

"Hey," Gage shouted. "Stop that, you asshole."

Simon whipped his head toward Gage. "Son of a bitch. There you are. Don't try anything with me. I know all about you, and you're not going to hurt Katy."

"Of course I'm not going to hurt her. What the hell are you doing? Coming out here—"

"Murderer," Simon shrieked.

Gage's stomach fell.

Simon stomped forward, his hands balled into fists. "Did some looking into you, mystery man. Think you can come in here and steal my woman?"

"She's not your woman. I didn't steal—" Gage jerked aside to avoid the fist Simon threw at him.

"Stop, Simon." Katy stood on the front porch, shouting a warning. "Leave. I called the police."

"Good. They can take away this murderer and keep you safe." Simon attempted to dodge past Gage only to be caught by the shoulder and whipped around.

"Don't go near her," Gage ordered.

"Or what? You'll kill me too? Did you tell Katy about that? How you killed your own father?"

Stunned by the words, Gage never saw it coming. Pain exploded in his jaw as Simon's fist connected with his face. Pain shot through his mind as what Simon was shrieking registered as well.

All the air rushed from his gut as Simon landed another blow. Gage folded around the other man's fist as he attempted to break free. He lashed out at Simon, fists and forearms meeting, the icy-cold air around them clouding as Simon continued to scream insults.

Gage saved his breath, backing up enough to get the space he needed to strike. A new kind of pain blossomed, this time in his knuckles as his fist connected with Simon's face and sent him staggering.

The world slowed to here and now. Gage's ribs and face took a beating as he worked to keep Simon from approaching the house any farther. He wasn't trying to take the man down, but to protect Katy. Or at least that was his main motivation. He couldn't deny the small part inside pleased to be inflicting pain on his rival.

The headlights spotlighted their macabre dance.

"You plan on hurting Katy, you're going to have to go through me." Simon lunged forward and drove Gage to the ground.

Snow stuck instantly to his bare arms and the back of his neck, but he was more worried about flying fists. He roared as he reared upward, slamming a hand against Simon's chest and exchanging their positions. One more blow to Simon's face and the man rolled to protect himself. Gage used the momentum to flip Simon to his stomach, then scrambled on top and trapped Simon's hands behind his back.

Gage paused, breathing heavily. Ready to do more, but willing to stop as long as Simon didn't move an inch. "Stay put until the police get here."

Simon glared, his one cheek shoved into the snowy ground. He was red-eyed and furious, and alcohol fumes rose off him in waves. "Killed your own father. You think I'm going to allow my kid anywhere near you?"

"Shut up," Gage ordered.

Sirens whistled in the background, growing closer.

Simon raised his voice. "Ask him, Katy. Ask him what happened to his dad. Then ask yourself if you should be with him or me. I love you, Katy. I'll take care of you."

Gage resisted the urge to stuff Simon's mouth with snow, instead adjusting position and making sure Simon's hands were firmly pinned in place.

Two RCMP cruisers pulled into the yard, sirens silenced but the red and blue lights on top flashing a mad display. The officers raced up about the time Katy's dad arrived from his rooms above the garage.

Voices and shouting continued. A whirl of motion and forceful commands. Gage backed off Simon, holding his hands in the air to reassure the cops.

"He attacked me," Simon roared. "Make sure he doesn't go near Katy. I'm telling you, he's a killer."

His shouts only cut off when he was finally stuffed into the back of a RCMP cruiser, and the door closed on him.

Two officers broke apart from the others to return to Gage. One wore a familiar face. Anna Coleman. Hard to believe one of the kids he'd gone to school with was now part of the local police force.

She looked him over carefully. "You okay?"

"I'm fine."

She glanced up at the house, then back at her team. "We'll get their statements. You take Simon in."

KATY'S FEET WERE FREEZING, but she wasn't moving from her position on the front porch until Gage was back in the house and Simon was gone. Hopefully to hell.

Her father wrapped an arm around her. "Come on, baby. Come inside. It won't help anything if you get sick."

She still waited just inside the door until an officer led Gage into the house. He was bleeding from a cut along his jaw, but throwing herself into his arms and clinging tight was as necessary as breathing.

Gage clutched her to himself, whispering soothingly as he stroked her hair. "It's okay. He's gone, and you're safe."

He repeated it over and over, as if reassuring himself.

Anna interrupted with a soft cough. "I need to find out what happened."

Katy refused to let go of Gage's hand, sitting next to him on the couch while her dad settled in a chair to one side. Gage repeated what had happened, and Anna took notes, her partner leaving the room to examine the bedroom at one point.

"You have any contact with Simon in the past few days?" she asked Katy once the initial questions were over.

She shook her head. "I told him last month that until there was some proof of paternity, I wasn't interested in a relationship with him anymore."

"What about you, Gage? Any contact or trouble?" Anna asked.

Gage paused for so long Katy stiffened. Had something happened she didn't know about? But it was a completely different track Gage rushed down.

"I haven't seen him, but there's some bad blood between us. We've had a few clashes before."

"Enough that he'd accuse you of potentially hurting Katy?"

"I think he went looking back into my history." His fingers around hers tightened as he turned to face her. "When my dad went crazy and started hitting my mom, I didn't know what to do. I remember rushing up and shouting at him, trying to get him to stop, but he was so furious, he wasn't hearing anything. He backhanded me hard enough I got knocked aside."

He wouldn't meet her eyes, staring at the floor as he continued. "I couldn't stop him, but I couldn't let him keep hurting her, so I ran to the truck. His gun was in the window rack, and I grabbed it, thinking the sight of it might

139

scare him off. But he ignored me, and when my mom started screaming, I...I swung at him, using the gun like a club."

Katy's fingers had gone as icy cold as the rest of her. "What happened?"

Gage ignored the RCMP sitting across from them, ignored her father listening to every word. Focused completely on her as if willing her to understand. "He wouldn't stop hitting her, Katy. Even after the first time I hit him with the gunstock. So I swung again, and again, until he turned his attention off her and onto me. Only then I already had the gun in motion, and it hit him in the side of the head. He finally went down. It was an accident, but it wasn't, because I wish I would have done it sooner to have given my mom a chance."

Keith Thompson swore lightly. "And that killed him?"

Gage nodded.

Katy sat silently for a moment, trying to take it in. No one spoke. No one moved.

He lifted his head, and his eyes were haunted.

"None of this is on your record, correct?" Anna asked.

"No. It went through the juvenile courts, and it was also considered self-defense, but it doesn't change the fact. Simon wasn't lying about that one part—I did kill my father."

The RCMP took more notes, asked more questions, but Katy's brain kept repeating on an endless loop the story Gage had shared, tonight and a month ago. So much sadness he'd had to endure at such a young age. Such a horrifying and violent loss.

Gage touched her arm and she jerked upright with a gasp.

"Sorry, but they asked you a question."

"Do you want me to start an emergency restraining order against Simon?" Anna asked.

Sheer relief rushed her. "Whatever it takes so I don't have to see him again."

Anna nodded. "I'll get things together for you. Come by the office first thing in the morning. I assume you'll press charges for tonight?"

"Definitely." Keith Thompson spoke up. "If you need anything regarding that, contact me."

The RCMP left first. Keith disappeared briefly only to come back shaking his head. "You kids can't stay here. Go to Gage's—I'll cover the windows, and we'll clean the rest tomorrow."

If she'd been numb before, by the time they were at Gage's place Katy was a walking zombie, only every time she tried to relax she heard glass shattering or Simon shouting.

Gage pulled her closer as they lay in his bed. "You want a hot drink or something to help you relax?"

She shook her head, not sure if he could see it in the dark. "Nothing."

He stroked her back softly, trying to soothe her. He had to be hurting from the punches Simon had gotten in, but he didn't say a word about it. He focused on something different. "I'm sorry I didn't tell you the entire story before."

God. "I understand it would have been tough to talk about, and I'm not mad. I'm just sorry Simon went crazy like that tonight—it must have been terrible for you."

"I was worried about you."

She squeezed him hard. "I know, but...I'm sorry if it brought back bad memories. Of your mom and dad."

"Oh, Katy." He kissed her tenderly. "That's the least of my concerns right now. I'm a grown-up and I've moved on. I was afraid that I might have my father's temper, but I've chosen to be different. I'm not afraid to fight to defend someone I care about, but I won't go too far."

Confusion and fear and exhaustion mixed together, and made her brain more tangled than clear. "I'm not even sure what I'm saying anymore, except I hate that I was the cause of a fight."

He curled himself around her, but his body had tightened. "I'll never sit back and allow you to be hurt, Katy. I'm going to protect you, no matter what the cost to me."

Her throat tightened at the enormousness of that statement.

A strange sensation hit her belly. She slipped her hands down, tilting her hips back slightly to be able to cup the growing baby.

"Katy, you okay?"

"Wait..."

It happened again, and she wasn't sure if she was about to laugh or cry. "The baby moved."

Gage's much-bigger hand slid over hers as their voices stilled, and she waited for another nudge from within. Silence surrounded them until all she heard was their even breathing and the light buzz from the distant refrigerator.

A faint motion. Rolling or wiggling. Now that the sensation had repeated, she realized this wasn't the first time. What changed was her awareness of her baby making itself known. She shifted her hand out of the way to direct Gage's palm directly over the most active spot.

Gage held his breath. Another flutter went off, and he made a noise. "That's... Wow."

His huge hand that lay so tenderly over her belly had been curled into a fist to defend her only an hour earlier. Strength and softness. Power and control.

A shiver rocked her at the anger Simon had shown—how out of control and dangerous he'd been.

Gage adjusted position, spooning her back into his warmth, instinctively knowing she needed the comfort. "I'll take care of you, Katy. You and the baby."

Katy clung to his words, fighting the lingering fear that they hadn't seen the last of their troubles.

CHAPTER 15

Timing for the May long-weekend fair and picnic was nearly perfect. Local ranchers and farmers were done enough of the spring planting to take a moment and actually relax. The rest of Rocky Mountain House that could shut down for part of the day did, and the weather usually cooperated.

It was one of Katy's favourite community events. Like hibernating animals crawling from their dens to discover the world had become shiny and fresh all over again.

She was more like a bloated balloon than a thin blade of spring grass, but getting to ditch the heavy winter coat and boots at least made her a few pounds lighter. The baby was taking up more and more room in the bulkhead that had become her stomach, but her changing body didn't bother her too much. The kid needed room to grow, yet the timing for her due date meant she wouldn't be hauling a huge belly around all hot, sweaty summer long.

Or maybe best of all? Gage didn't seem to mind one bit. He'd been attentive and caring, and oh-my-gawd intensely involved for the last three months.

She'd been surprised when her interest in sex hadn't decreased as her girth widened, but maybe the nonstop caresses and massages had something to do with that.

He'd all but moved in with her. Fixed the damages caused by Simon then they'd both set out to ignore the other man. The restraining order had been a sad but necessary step.

Gage paced beside her, his fingers linked through hers as they strolled the fairgrounds, the scent of buttery popcorn and new-mown grass mixing into a sort of holiday-themed perfume.

"Move over, dude." Janey shoved her way between them, linking her hands over both their elbows. "I take it we won't be attempting any ride records on the Zipper this year, hey, Katy?"

Oh, lordy, no. "I can only imagine what that would do to the kid. If you want to challenge your stomach, sweet-talk someone else into riding with you."

Janey squeezed her arm. "Perfect. That's what I hoped you'd say."

She stepped forward, boldly tugging Gage with her.

"Hey." He resisted her takeover. "Not me."

Katy laughed. "Go on if you want to. I'll wander for a bit."

"Nope. I'm here with you," Gage insisted. His eyes lit with mischief. "Hey, Len. You still scared of heights?"

Her brother sauntered into view, corndog in one hand, burger in the other. "You smoking something funny over here? I'm not afraid of heights."

"Good to hear." Gage darted a quick glance at Katy. "Then you can take Janey on the Zipper."

Janey dug her fingers into Gage's side briefly, and Katy attempted not to laugh out loud. She joined him in the

VIVIAN AREND

tease, complete seriousness in her voice. "That's a good idea. I usually ride with her, but this year the poor girl is simply lost without me."

"With friends like you two, who needs enemies?" Janey muttered. Then she turned her bright smile on Len. "So, whad'ya say? Shall we go flip ourselves around and show the teenagers how it's done?"

Len gave them a dirty look before gesturing Janey ahead of him toward the fair rides set up in the corner of the grounds.

Katy and Gage managed to wait until the other two were out of hearing range before bursting into laughter. "That was sheer brilliance," Katy praised him.

Gage caught her fingers in his. "Len likes her. I don't know what his problem is."

"Janey's a bit...exuberant at times. Bet they'll figure it out eventually." Katy got sidetracked by the sight of an art display. "Come on, I want to look closer at this."

One of the locals who had an art studio had displays of her work set up on easels, and Katy slipped in closer to chat with Ashley for a while. The other woman had far more experience, with an art show or two under her belt. Katy loved that there were people she could turn to for help as her new interests continued to grow.

Gage let her go, striding over to the next tent where a group of guys had gathered to shoot the breeze.

Ashley smiled. "Hey, good to see you again. Name is Ashley if you've lost it."

Katy accepted a brief hug. "You're so lovely. Also, thank you for not saying, 'Haven't you had that baby yet?' People should have to give me a quarter every time they mutter that phrase."

"You're not ready to pop," Ashley teased.

"Four weeks left." Katy admired the painting in front of her, with two cowboys sitting easily on the backs of their horses. "Your work is amazing."

The woman grinned harder. "I have great inspiration."

They both turned without a word to stare across the yard. Katy took a moment to admire Ashley's men, Travis and Cassidy, but her gaze moved quickly to Gage. "I'll say. I think I need to suggest another practice session of nude sketches. To work on my anatomy lines."

Ashley chuckled. "Dirty girl. I knew I liked you for a reason."

They exchanged smiles then visited for a bit longer before Katy wandered off. Gage was still busy talking to his friends, so she waited outside the cookhouse and chatted with the ladies there. Familiar faces—at times names eluded her, but her problem didn't bother her nearly so much anymore.

The people who mattered knew how to help her, and the people who didn't know, she got around.

Life had changed a lot since the previous fall. The kid rolling awkwardly inside her was only part of it as elbows or knees dug into her bladder at the most inopportune moments.

It was bigger things. She was more confident than she used to be. More determined to do what was right for her and the baby. More in tune with the man who had come into her life in a powerful way.

HE WATCHED HER. All the time Gage laughed and joked with his friends, he kept an eye on Katy. Loving the moments where she smiled in response to a comment, her entire face shining with happiness and joy.

He got to see her like that more often these days, and her enthusiasm thrilled him.

A hand clamped down on his shoulder. "You're obsessed with my sister," Clay poked.

"Not even going to deny it."

Clay grumbled. "No fun to tease you anymore. You're all Katy all the time."

"Tease Mitch instead," Troy suggested. "He's got a cop on his tail. One more ticket, bro, and she's going to impound your bike and slap your ass in jail for a couple nights."

Mitch didn't answer, just eyed Anna Coleman as she strolled through the crowd patrolling the fair grounds, her uniform far more wrinkled than usual. Gage wondered briefly if something was going on he wasn't aware of.

He'd been so focused on Katy and his conversation that he almost missed it. A familiar face popped out briefly from behind the corner of the cookhouse.

"Was that Simon?" he snapped.

Clay twirled. "Where? He's not supposed to be anywhere near Katy."

There was no one there. "I'm seeing things," Gage mumbled.

Only he still left the tent, glancing around closely. He passed Len and Janey returning from the rides, Janey's cheeks flushed from excitement.

She slowed as he passed her. "Gage? What's up?"

He ignored her, pacing forward. Fucker. It *was* Simon, now leaning on the outside of the cookhouse and staring intently at Katy. The expression on Simon's face suggested his attention wasn't a good thing.

"Oh my God, that's Simon." Janey slapped Gage on the

shoulder rapidly a dozen times, her voice shaking as she ran along beside him. "What's he doing here? What's he doing?"

Gage wasn't going to wait for something bad to happen. He stormed across the clearing between tents, headed straight for the troublemaker. He grabbed Simon by the back of the shirt and jerked him off his feet. "What the hell? You're not welcome here."

Simon scrambled to free himself from Gage's grip, seams shredding as he broke free and stumbled into the crowd. He used the people around him to pull himself upright and whirl toward Gage.

"Bastard," he snarled. "You think you're so much better than me, but you're the biggest loser here. A liar and a killer, and you don't deserve to be with someone like Katy."

Gage lifted his fists and widened his stance. Simon wanted a fight? Bring it on.

Janey slipped into his peripheral vision, standing well back from them both. "Gage. I called the police and they'll be—"

"Police? What the fuck did you do that for?" Panic streaked across Simon's face, and he surged forward, only this time toward Katy, one hand raised threateningly in the air.

"Katy, watch out," Janey shouted.

Gage lost it. He threw himself in front of Katy as a protective wall, and Simon bounced off him.

"Back off," Gage warned.

Simon exploded, punishing Gage with a flurry of fists. He wrapped an arm around Gage and jolted forward, the two of them staggering into the crowd as people screamed and attempted to run away. Katy cried out, his name escaping her in pained gasp.

The sound barreled through him, a terrifying echo from his past when he'd been too late to make a difference.

Gage went numb.

Katy. He had to protect Katy.

Simon wasn't supposed to be here, not this close to Katy, but the man obviously didn't care about the law. Gage ignored the fist smashing against his face, instead pushed forward and did his best to move Simon farther from his target. Pain ignored, the shimmer of stars floating past his eyes ignored. All that mattered was keeping Katy safe.

Around them people continued to shout, but Gage didn't stop. Didn't stop until he was on the ground, and even then he clutched Simon tightly, refusing to allow the man to escape.

He didn't swing his fists—didn't attack. Just held on and took the assault as he kept Simon away from Katy.

"Gage, you ass, let him go," Clay shouted from somewhere close by.

The shouting and noise seemed to be dropping, but the adrenaline racing through him kept his grip firm. "No, he'll hurt Katy."

"No one is going to hurt Katy." Clay's big hands pushed down on his shoulders. "Jeez, man. The RCMP are right here. Let him go so they don't rip off his arms."

Gage relaxed. Simon was lifted off him, rapidly pulled to his feet and away from where Gage remained on the ground.

Clay offered a hand and pulled him upright, bracing him for a moment as everything spun. Gage's eyes wouldn't focus for a minute, and he blinked hard. "Katy. Where's Katy?" he demanded.

"Settle down," Clay ordered. "She's over there."

Gage whipped his head to check she was okay, nearly

falling over he moved so fast. "Thank God, you're safe. You okay?"

Her face had gone white, and her hands were draped protectively around her belly. She nodded, leaning against Janey as her friend pulled her into a hug.

A few feet away Anna Coleman stood guarding a hand-cuffed Simon. Her partner Nick stood beside Gage, while other RCMP worked to calm the crowd.

"I'll be back in a minute." Anna Coleman spoke softly. "Gage, don't leave before we talk to you, understand?"

Gage nodded, and Anna turned to lead Simon to the police car.

Nick interrupted her departure. "Wait. I hate to do this in light of what just happened, but I have no choice."

He reached into his jacket and pulled out a long envelope, passing it to Gage.

This wasn't the time. "I need to see Katy," Gage protested.

Nick forced the paper into his hand. "Read it, now," he ordered.

"You had it coming," Simon gloated. "Stay away from my woman, Jenick."

Oh shit. That couldn't be good. Gage ripped the top off the envelope and frantically opened the paper. The words made no sense, though. "This... This can't be right."

He had to be seeing things.

"What is it?" Katy asked, stepping closer.

Nick held up a hand, undeniable reluctance twisting his expression. "I'm sorry, Katy. You can't come any closer than that, I'm afraid."

Gage held the papers to Clay. "Did Simon hit me harder than I thought? How can this be legal?"

It was Nick who answered. "They were delivered this morning."

"It's for your own safety, Katy." Simon had put on the act again, all calm and mature, as if he hadn't just tried to attack her. "For our baby."

Nick motioned to Anna. "Take him away, I'll deal with this."

Everyone fell silent as a laughing Simon was guided off the fairgrounds, Anna Coleman's firm grip on his shoulder.

Gage's gaze met Katy's—her panic and upset so clear he nearly ignored everyone around them and stomped across the space separating them, papers be damned.

"Gage? What's going on?" she asked.

Clay walked over to give his sister the papers, wrapping an arm around her. The expression on Katy's face as she read them scared him more than the sight of Simon stalking her had.

"It's a restraining order against Gage," Nick explained to Katy. "Using Gage's history, Simon went in front of a judge and filed a complaint. He said he had concerns that you and your baby might be in danger, especially if it's discovered that the baby is actually his."

"That's bullshit," Janey snapped. "How can Simon get a restraining order on Gage? That's up to Katy, not anyone else."

Nick shook his head. "Except in special circumstances. Here in Alberta, this is a civil-court matter. If there's a reasonable belief that a claim is valid, exceptions can be made. The judge agreed there was a possibility of danger considering Gage was involved in a violent incident as a youth."

"Violent incident...? He was trying to save his mom."

Katy shook the papers. "This is wrong, and the only reason Simon did it was to control me and hurt Gage."

Nick sighed. "There's nothing I can do. Gage can go in front of a judge to protest, but until it's overruled, the order stands until the baby is born and the paternity test is complete."

Clay was back by Gage's side, offering support. Gage rested a hand on his friend's shoulder, the world swirling between pain and frustration.

Fear still shone in Katy's eyes, and Gage felt it to his very soul. "I can't be with Katy?"

"I'm sorry, no. No contact over the phone or Internet either. No communication. It's a full restriction, and if you break it, you can be arrested."

Gage wanted to shout in rage even though that was the worst possible idea at the moment. Fury against Simon shot through him like living flames, but his hands were tied.

He was trapped.

Across from him, Katy faced Nick. "I need to talk to you for a minute."

The RCMP looked confused, but he nodded. "Go on."

She spoke clearly, her voice the only sound as everyone around them hushed to silence once more. "Simon went too far. I'm going to do everything possible to make sure he gets no contact with my baby, even if he is the biological dad. He's dangerous."

Sweet relief poured through Gage.

Her voice quivered for a second, those beautiful eyes of hers filling with tears, but she still lifted her chin and continued. "Tell Gage not to break the order. Contact the judge to see if he can get it lifted, but if he can't, I want him to wait it out. It's only for a little while. It sucks and it's wrong, and if Simon were still here I'd be the first one to knock him on his ass for doing this to us, but it's not worth going to jail for. I'll be fine, and within a month we'll be past this and we'll go on with our lives."

Such strength and power in her small frame, Gage was nearly overwhelmed by the display. "Hey, Nick?" he called.

The RCMP turned his way. "Yes?"

Gage followed Katy's lead. "Tell Katy I'm going to do everything I can."

"I know…" she answered, not looking away from Nick.

Nick shook his head. "Guys, you have to stop this. It's time to move on."

They faced each other across the distance that before had seemed like nothing but was now as large a barrier as the Atlantic Ocean. Tears streaked down her cheeks as she gazed sorrowfully one final time before walking toward the parking lot.

Gage's soul crumbled into dust. "How could this happen?" he whispered. "It's not right, to leave her all alone. I wanted to protect her. I *need* to protect her…"

The murmur of voices rose as Janey stepped to his side. She laid her hand on his arm. "I'll go with her. I know it's not what you really want, but somehow we'll get through this."

"Go—" he urged.

Janey quick-stepped across the field to rejoin Katy, slipping an arm around her. Katy leaned her head on her friend's shoulder, and they walked slowly, disappearing from sight around the corner.

All the happiness and joy Gage had finally allowed himself to grasp slipped away like ashes being blown from an abandoned fire pit.

CHAPTER 16

K aty stared into her backyard. The garden gnomes had been at it again.

Well, one gnome of unusually large size.

For the past week since the picnic, Gage had taken to showing up and doing her chores. Silently. He didn't try to speak to her, but every morning before heading to work he arrived and did something that needed to be done. Chopped wood and stockpiled it for the winter. Weeded the garden. Turned over another section along the fence where she'd mentioned planting raspberry canes.

He came back in the evenings to move sprinklers and deal with the trash. It was tortuous to see him, and want him, and not be able to touch him.

Maybe they could have cheated and gotten together. Phoned or emailed or even had him sneak into the house in the dark. She wasn't about to turn him in, and neither was her family. But it would only take one misunderstanding to blow the entire thing up around them. Katy stuck with what she'd told him originally. They could handle the separation for the short time required.

No communication. No contact. No coming closer than the prearranged distance.

Instead, Clay stopped by to tell her the latest news from Gage. The judge he'd gone to see had been sympathetic but insisted the concerns raised were valid enough to take seriously. The order stayed in place.

Simon was behind bars for breaking his own restraining order. Katy couldn't have handled not having Gage around and knowing Simon was roaming free.

Only as she wandered the house, the baby weighing heavier all the time, it was lonely. Heartbreaking, body-achingly lonely.

This was more frustrating than the days immediately after her memory loss the previous fall. At least then she had forgotten about the things that had made her sad as well as the things that had made her happy. Now she knew what would make her happy, but she was helpless to reach out and grab it.

Helpless to give that happiness back to Gage as well.

Her dad showed up one night, staring out at the yard while Gage was there. Usually didn't say much, her dad. So when he spoke, she listened.

"Remember the first time I met Gage. Kind of looked lost." Keith Thompson fidgeted with a set of crayons she'd left on the table. "Took a long time for that kid to smile. I mean, really smile. Almost seemed something inside him had been rusted shut, and turning the lock to open it was painful. But he did get there. Eventually."

Her dad eased himself up off the chair and paused, still staring outside. "Seen him more than smile because of you, Katy. You make him shine bright like your mama used to make me come alive inside. He's a good man. You'll get through this, and in the end it'll be worth it." He kissed her cheek before leaving. She was torn between crying and laughing, and ended up doing a strange combination of both that left her sniffling through hiccups.

And now her backyard was awash in a sea of blue.

All along the perimeter, where the fence created too much shade for anything much to grow, low-lying plants full of tiny blue flowers covered every inch of ground. It was like someone had poured spectacular winter sky over the ground and it had set roots.

She pulled her robe over the extension of her belly the best she could, slipped on old shoes and stepped out into the fresh morning air. She paced the yard slowly, examining the plants as if they would somehow make all her problems go away.

They were beautiful, and she wanted to draw pictures of them, which was a totally irrational response to the fact that Gage Jenick had somehow overnight transformed her yard into a botanical wonderland.

There was no mistaking this for anyone else's work, especially not when she turned and discovered him standing at the edge of the fence. The fence he'd fixed a couple days earlier.

They stared across the yard at each for all of thirty seconds before he turned, ready to walk away.

"Wait." Katy glanced around. No one close, no one to tell... So irresistible.

Gage swallowed hard as she approached, holding up a hand as if to ward her off. "Stop."

She paused at the closest point legally possible, ignoring the fact that even talking was supposed to be out of bounds. "I had to see you."

He examined her closely like a man drinking deeply after a drought. "You okay?"

She nodded. "I've got this really great gardener."

Gage smiled, but it was a faint flicker of the old expression that could bring her to her knees with longing. As if he was holding back. Cautious. "Do you recognize them?" he asked, pointing to the flowers.

Keeping their discussion normal. Easy, and fit for public conversation. Not intimate, which was probably good or she'd be tempted to throw herself into his arms and damn the consequences. She twisted to check her backyard. "Flowers aren't my thing. Yet. Who knows what I'll pick up next, though. They're very pretty."

"They're called forget-me-nots. They'll fade after a few months, but they bloom every year just as bright as before. It's like..." he paused, "...for a little while they go to sleep, but they're always there. Waiting to show what they're really like inside."

A knife blade of emotion, painful and sharp, twisted in her belly.

He reached for her but let his hand fall away before they connected. Gage cleared his throat, staring over the field of flowing blue. "I miss you. Stay safe, okay?"

Then he turned and walked away, taking her heart with him.

CHAPTER 17

There was this itchy sensation at the back of her brain screaming it was past time for this to be over. Not only the baby's arrival, but *all* of it. Her family had taken control of the waiting room down the hall, but they still managed to hover. Between the anxious glances and the well-meant but annoying suggestions to make her feel better, she was ready to kick their collective oversized asses out of the hospital.

She was having a baby, damn it, not on her deathbed. There was too much going on now that labour had started. Too much, and yet not enough to distract her from thinking about what she wanted.

Or more specifically *who* she wanted.

"I can't do this anymore." Katy eased her way down the hall, holding tightly to Janey's arm.

"I don't think you can cancel at this point, hon." Janey paced slowly, her head dipping closer as her volume went even lower. "Although, if you want me to encourage anyone to leave, tell me, okay? Anyone," she said pointedly as one of Katy's brothers stepped toward them.

Here they went again. Katy eased a hand over her rock-solid belly as she paused to deal with another contraction. "Oh *damn*, this hurts."

Her brother Troy wrapped an arm around her shoulders. "You're doing great."

She couldn't answer for a moment. It was nice to know they cared, but really? Her brothers and her dad? Katy blew out the final moment of pain and straightened to look into Troy's concerned eyes. "Thanks for the encouragement, but please. Go home, and we'll let you know when the kid arrives."

"Take the other guys with you too," Janey suggested. "Because, dude, none of you are going anywhere near the delivery room when the actual event is happening."

"Ick, that is so true." Katy squeezed her brother's hand. "I'm glad you want to be there for me, but this is going a little too far, if you know what I mean."

Only, Troy wasn't watching her, he was watching the nurses' station. "I don't mind hanging out for a while."

Jeez, good to know his reasons for being here weren't all about wrapping her in cotton. "Go home, Troy. Or at least pretend to go so I don't have to look at you. We'll call when there's news."

Katy stepped away and ignored him, easing through the next few contractions.

It wasn't her family she wanted around. She wanted Gage. She'd allowed him to be sent way, and she'd thought it was the right thing to do, but now that the moment had come she wasn't so sure.

Janey led her down the corridors in an endless loop. Her brothers had at least obeyed the part about getting out of sight, although knowing them, they'd probably only hit the coffee shop on the second floor and were tormenting people there.

Between contractions and pacing, she paused to look out the window. Spring had already passed, easing into full-on summer, and it was time for all kinds of new things.

Maybe a new chance as well.

Janey leaned on the wall beside her, arms crossed over her chest. "You want to call him?"

Was she that transparent? "Gage?"

Her best friend shrugged. "Honey, you love the guy. I think he loves you, and I doubt at this point anyone here at the hospital is going to call the cops if he shows up, restraining order or not." She made a rude noise. "I think we'd all lie our asses off for you two right now."

"I can't..." Katy thought really hard about what she wanted to say to finish that sentence.

She couldn't what?

I can't do this without him.

She lifted her eyes to her friend's. "Do you think he wants to be here? Even if it might get him arrested?"

Janey held out her cell phone, Gage's number already up on the screen. "I bet he'd go through hell itself to be here if you asked."

It really wasn't that hard, hitting the button to make the call.

"Janey?" Gage sounded breathless. "Is she okay? Is the baby there? Tell me they're both fine."

His obvious concern had Katy's throat closing tight, and she had to force out the words. "Gage, it's me. I'm doing good, but..."

"Katy? Thank God. You had the baby?"

"Not yet." She paused, wondering if it was right to even

offer him the temptation. It wasn't her who could end up in jail.

But he'd told her once she should reach out and take what she wanted, and damn if she wasn't going to do exactly that. At least to offer him the option and let him decide if the risks were worth it. "This could get you in trouble, but do you want to be here? I mean, be with me when the baby arrives?"

"Oh, yeah." Loud clattering rang in the background, something like a door slamming. "Are you asking me to come to the hospital?"

"It might be a terrible idea, but yes, I want you here—oh, *shit*..." Another contraction hit, and she had to bend over and concentrate on breathing.

Gage's anxious voice blared from the phone as she held it against her thigh, his frantic questions getting louder and louder.

Janey somehow helped support her and at the same time grabbed the phone. "Stop shouting. She's busy for a minute." A pause, then Janey snorted. "Well, I don't know, sweetheart. Hold on to your knickers and I'll ask her."

Her friend held the phone against her chest to cover the speaker. "What should I tell him?"

Katy blew out a long breath as she found her feet, reaching for the phone. "Gage, me again. Sorry about that. I want you with me, if you still want to be here."

"You know I do."

Katy twisted to the right in surprise. His answer had come not from the phone, but from the man himself who stood only two feet away. He was breathing heavily as if he'd been running stairs.

Katy was breathing pretty hard herself. "Holy moly, how did you do that?"

"If he's got a transporter and he hasn't shared until now, I'm going to be pissed off." Janey held out her hand and gave Gage a quick handshake. "Now that you're here for backup, I'm going to do a little distracting of the nursing staff and warn the people who will help us. I'll return in a moment to be an awesome baby catcher. I suggest you two hide out in the birthing room."

"Good idea."

They paused as Janey backed away, briefly flashing them two thumbs-up before she twirled and disappeared around a corner. Gage let Katy guide him quickly into the private room she'd been given.

Only once the door was shut did he answer Katy's question. "I was in the parking lot, waiting in my truck. Hoping that you'd call."

He was there, the bruises on his face fading, his dark eyes taking her in from head to toe, and he reached out...

And stopped.

His hand fell to his side. His big strong body trembling as if he were afraid.

"Katy, I'm here for you. For you and the baby." His eyes —God, his *eyes*. Full of pain, and yet hope. "I promise with everything in me that's true."

She was going to be bawling in a minute, which wasn't going to work great with the whole labour thing still happening. "I know."

Katy caught him by the hand and tugged them together. She had to twist sideways to make room for her belly as she stepped into the warmth of his body, but he had his arms around her and that was all she needed right then. The solid assurance that he was there. That he was hers.

Gage stroked her hair as he held her. "I hate that we've had to be apart."

She nodded. "If you see the RCMP coming, hide in the bathroom."

A reluctant laugh escaped him. "No more hiding. This is too important an event for me to spend it in the parking lot waiting for news."

"Were you really just going to sit there?" Katy didn't want to let go of him, his touch soothing her more than any breathing techniques.

Gage stroked her cheek as he gazed into her eyes. "I was planning on sneaking in, but this is so much better than hiding behind a mask and staring through the door. And if I do get in trouble, it'll be worth it."

They had to pause each time a contraction hit, but the distraction of their conversation helped make the pain fade a little.

He rubbed her back before she even asked him to, touching her gently, supporting her. His strong hands that were capable of inflicting pain giving such tender care.

And when he cupped her face in his hands and leaned in to kiss her tenderly, she lost it.

"It was bad enough that I had to lose memories, now I've lost these last weeks with you." She held his hand against her cheek. "Damn Simon to hell."

"Forget Simon, Katybug. He doesn't matter, or he won't in a few days. What does matter is I love you."

She gasped out a laugh past the tears. "I love you too, Gage."

"Forever," he added, stroking her cheek and wiping away her tears. "I'm going to love you forever. And that's not going to change, and if I have to spend the next sixty years reminding you again and again, it'll be worth it."

"It'll be worth it," she repeated. There were still questions they had to answer, but right now, he was there and the kid in her belly was posing the most demanding request. "Ahh, Gage? I think it's time."

"Time for what?"

She wanted to laugh, but the pressure was building too fast. "The baby?" she reminded him.

His eyes widened. "Now?"

"Now."

AFTER THE CHAOS of the birth scene, quiet finally descended. Everywhere except in Gage's brain. Well, his heart—that too was going a million miles an hour, and the reason was right there in his hands.

The doctor had left after giving them a wink and placing his finger against his lips.

Janey had left.

Katy had stepped into the shower, and the nurse had pushed him back into the chair beside the bed. Without so much as a "here you go" she'd placed baby Tanner in his arms. Then she'd left the room, giving Gage no opportunity to do anything but sit there and stare at the tiny person he held cradled in his hands.

Honest truth? He was fucking scared to death. By a bundle of humanity the size of a bread loaf.

The baby boy wiggled, and Gage pulled him closer, soft flannel pressing the side of his arm as he cradled the bundle. "Oh, man. This is..."

The kid's face was all scrunched up—no way to tell family resemblance to anyone when he looked like that. Gage glanced around the room to double-check he was alone then carefully laid the baby in his lap and loosened off the blanket.

VIVIAN AREND

It might be stupid, but he had to see. He wasn't looking for a distinguishing mark or anything, but...

Gage wanted to count toes. And fingers. And look again at how perfectly human, and yet perfectly tiny the baby was.

Tanner complained loudly about being poked and prodded. His arms flared out, fists waving in the air, and Gage did his best to rewrap him. The trick eluded him, and things were a bit of a mess, but Tanner settled down, his bright blue eyes seeming to stare straight through Gage.

"So. You're here."

Another thing that might be stupid, but it felt right to talk to the kid. Tell him...

"You know, your mom is pretty incredible. You have no idea what she just went through for you. Frankly, you probably don't want to know, but right off the bat, you picked a good one, kid. She's loved you with everything in her since she knew you were coming, and she wants nothing but the best for you."

The words stuck in his throat for a minute as that really, truly registered. How much Katy loved Tanner. The fact she'd said she loved Gage as well?

It wasn't as if there was a limit to love. Only so much to be doled out a little at a time before you had to hold back and save some for another day.

The baby lying in his lap was proof that love wasn't about what you could do, or where you'd come from. Love was a gift, and damn if emotion wasn't welling up in a way that made Gage gasp at the sharpness of it cutting away the bloody edges inside.

Did it really matter if Tanner was the result of his genes and Katy's mixing? Or did it matter more that Gage would be called *daddy*? That he could be a father Tanner looked up to—he'd teach his son to do all the fun things in life, and to deal with all the responsibilities, but most of all he could teach his son how to love unconditionally.

If it turned out Simon had started this life, and the courts decreed he had to be involved, Gage would find a way to make sure even that was somehow a positive experience. He'd protect Tanner, like he would protect Katy going forward. Not with fists and violence, but in a way that would make a difference in the end.

God, somehow, he would find a way.

"So, here's the deal. I'm your daddy. Well, I need to do some convincing to get your mom to marry me before it will be official, but whatever else happens, or however long that takes, you and me? We're the real deal. We're going to be having a lot of talks over the years. About doing chores you hate, and girls you like. And maybe we'll talk about cars or computers or whatever else comes along. But I'm going to be there for you. For you and your momma. And it doesn't matter to me one bit if you're someone else's son, because you're mine, and I'm so damn thankful for you."

He had to wipe away a tear. "Not at all what I expected, but it's exactly what I needed—you coming into my life. And maybe we'll fight at times, or you'll get grounded—hell, I kind of expect you will if you're anything like me—but no matter what, I'm your daddy. And that's never going to change."

He'd been so intent on the pain that was leaving him in a rush he hadn't noticed the shower had turned off.

The first thing that registered was the soft touch of hands slipping over his shoulders as Katy draped herself up against his back. She touched her cheek to his, moisture connecting—his tears or hers?

She snuck a hand around his torso and laid her fingers

over his where he gently held Tanner. "I love you, Gage. We'll find a way."

"We'll make memories, good ones, and we'll find a way," he agreed.

He opened his arms and pulled them in close. Opened his heart and did the same. This wasn't about his past, it was about his future. A grown-up, straight-up heart-and-brain decision to be there for the two people who mattered the most. His lover.

And his son.

CHAPTER 18

Five days later

The test results came sealed in an envelope. One page, with all kinds of numbers and details at the bottom, but all Gage could see through his tears was the beginning.

The results of the paternity test are consistent with the alleged father GAGE MICHAEL JENICK being the biological father of the child TANNER NATE THOMPSON. The probability of paternity is greater than 99.9%.

EPILOGUE

Katy took another box off the shelf, peeking inside briefly before abandoning it with the others. In the background, she heard the sounds of water splashing, and a momentary protest rang out as Tanner squawked. Gage's answer came immediately, soft and reassuring as he soothed the baby.

It was one of the wonderful parts of being a family. Gage had taken over the nighttime bath routine, leaving her a few moments to accomplish something without the little one around.

Tonight she'd grown serious enough to venture into the storage room. She'd created a one-of-a-kind scrapbook to record Tanner's milestones—crafted together from a hardcover book Janey had gifted her and some of her new artistic talent. The details were caught up, but now she wanted to compare it to what was recorded in her own baby book.

Only where was it?

She pulled the lid off yet another box, surprised to find the decorative book that used to sit beside her computer. She'd used it for taking notes and jotting down recipes, and as she flipped through the pages realized she had stashed a backup of all her passwords.

Driven by curiosity, she tucked the book under her arm and headed down the hall, pausing in the door of the bathroom to watch her guys. Gage carefully washed Tanner's hair chatting all the time about engines and torque, and other things that made her smile. The baby did nothing more than gurgle in response, but Gage didn't seem to care.

He must've sensed she was there, and he glanced over his shoulder momentarily, his smile ratcheting up a notch as he looked her over.

"Well, whatever you're doing I look forward to joining you later." He leered at her, his hands carefully guarding Tanner as their son wiggled his limbs happily.

Katy stuck out her tongue and twirled away, the short shorts and tight tank top she was wearing to beat the August heat clinging to her body with a slick of sweat.

She sat at the computer and went to her long-since-abandoned email account. Stared at the password sign-in and wondered if it was even worthwhile. She loved Gage, trusted him. That wasn't even a question anymore. The only reason to look would be to satisfy her curiosity.

She really should go wash up the dinner dishes instead. Or clean up the mess she'd made with the new set of paints Gage had bought her to explore another artsy area that had caught her interest.

Curiosity won.

She checked the information in the flowery notebook, inserted the proper password, then hit enter.

The entire screen bloomed with unread emails. She rolled her eyes and scrolled back through months' worth of spam. It wasn't until she reached the previous October that there were some real emails for her, most of them containing information she had received after her accident. Information that had been duplicated and sent to her new account.

She knew the date she was looking for. By this time it wasn't a case of need to see it, but it was strangely comforting all the same that the email Gage had told her he had sent was there. She clicked it open and smiled, her heart filling with even more love as she read it through.

There was no room for sadness. No room for regrets that her accident had taken some of this from her. No room for anger at the lies Simon had told, first in insisting they'd gotten back together and then his manipulation toward the end.

As the sounds of her laughing husband and a contented baby carried into the main room, Katy had nothing inside but happiness. Filled to the top with love for two people, one of whom hadn't even existed this time last year.

She paused to print out the note, though. Not to show to Gage, but to slip into the other memory book she'd started. The one where she'd pinned the picture Gage had taken immediately after their first *official* kiss. The book she'd taped the ticket stubs from their first movie. Pasted the PG sketch she'd done of him—the dirty one she had tucked elsewhere to keep it from anyone else's eyes.

The printout was a new memory of the truth and commitment he'd offered her, even before she'd known how much she was going to need him.

Gage stepped back into the living room, Tanner in his arms. "Someone is ready for a cuddle."

He lowered their baby into her embrace then stepped back only far enough to drape his arm around her shoulders as he leaned against her, their bodies close and intimate.

Scrubbed and clean, eyes drooping with sleep, Tanner

stared up at them both, little mouth opening wide with a yawn.

"He's so gorgeous." Katy slipped a finger over his tiny lips, and he puckered, looking for something more.

"Of course he is. He's our kid." Gage reached over and tucked his finger into Tanner's tiny fist. Baby fingers barely reached around, but the kid hung on tight.

The soft touch of lips against her temple as Gage kissed her was the final blessing on the moment. Katy tucked herself and Tanner tighter into the embrace then looked up into the sincere gaze of her lover. The father of her child, in not just blood but all the more important ways.

"I love you, Gage Jenick. Heart and soul."

His grin widened. "I love you too, and you'd better never forget it."

She laughed as he turned her to face the backyard where he'd planted so many flowers. The brilliant blue flower petals had faded, but the message remained.

As his arms circled both of them, Katy leaned back and soaked in the wonder that was her life. The one full of memories with even more to be made in the future.

New York Times Bestselling Author Vivian Arend brings you a sexy and emotional series set in the foothills of the Alberta Rockies. Meet the Thompsons—five siblings with secrets and dreams. Join them as each member of this tight-knit family discovers love.

Thompson & Sons
Ride Baby Ride
Rocky Ride
One Sexy Ride
Let It Ride
A Wild Ride

ABOUT THE AUTHOR

With over 2.5 million books sold, Vivian Arend is a New York Times and USA Today bestselling author of over 60 contemporary and paranormal romance books, including the Six Pack Ranch and Granite Lake Wolves.

Her books are all standalone reads with no cliffhangers. They're humorous yet emotional, with sexy-times and happily-ever-afters. Vivian pretty much thinks she's got the best job in the world, and she's looking forward to giving readers more HEAs. She lives in B.C. Canada with her husband of many years and a fluffy attack Shih-tzu named Luna who ignores everyone except when treats are deployed.

www.vivianarend.com

Made in the USA
Middletown, DE
12 April 2024

52935196R00111